COUNTERFEIT
ELVIS
(WELCOME TO MY WORLD)

COUNTERFEIT ELVIS:
(Welcome To My World)

Copyright © 2013 by Raymond D. Mason

All rights reserved. No part of this book may be used or reproduced by any means, graphic, electronic, or mechanical; including photocopying, recording, taping or by any information storage retrieval system without the written permission of the publisher/author except in the case of brief quotations embodied in critical articles and reviews.

Raymond D. Mason books may be ordered through authorized booksellers associated with Mason Books or by contacting:

You may order books through:
www.Amazon.com
www.CreateSpace.com
www.BarnesandNoble.com
www.Target.com
or personalized autographed copies from:
E-mail: RMason3092@aol.com

(541) 679-0396

This is a work of fiction. All characters, names, incidents, organizations, and dialogue in this novel are either the products of the author's imagination or are used fictitiously.

Printed in the United States of America

Books by this Author

Mysteries

8 Seconds to Glory
A Motive for Murder
A Tale of Tri-Cities
A Walk on the Wilder Side
Beyond Missing
Blossoms in the Dust
Brotherhood of the Cobra
Corrigan
Counterfeit Elvis:
(Welcome to My World)*
If Looks Could Kill
Illegal Crossing
In the Chill of the Night
Most Deadly Intentions
Murder on the Oregon Express
Odor in the Court
On a Lonely Mountain Road
Return of 'Booger' Doyle
Send in the Clones
Shadows of Doubt
Sleazy Come, Sleazy Go
Suddenly, Murder
The Mystery of Myrtle Creek
The Secret of Spirit Mountain
The Tootsie Pop Kid
The Woman in the Field
Too Late To Live

Westerns

Aces and Eights
Across the Rio Grande
Beyond the Great Divide
Beyond the Picket Wire
Brimstone; End of the Trail
Day of the Rawhiders
Four Corners Woman
Incident at Medicine Bow
King of the Barbary Coast
Laramie
Last of the Long Riders
Night of the Blood Red Moon
Night Riders
Purple Dawn
Rage at Del Rio
Rebel Pride
Return to Cutter's Creek
Ride the Hard Land
Ride the Hellfire Trail
Showdown at Lone Pine
Streets of Durango: *Lynching*
Streets of Durango: *Shootings*
Tales of Old Arizona
The Long Ride Back
Three Days to Sundown
Yellow Sky, Black Hawk

Preface

This book is purely fiction and in no way intended to present the idea that any of the events were based on facts. I have been an Elvis Presley fan since I first heard him in 1956, so it is in no way intended to be a slam against the man, his music, his family, or his life in any stretch of the imagination.

It was while I was watching the Elvis movie 'Kissin' Cousins' that I got the idea for this story. Seeing Elvis playing a double role reminded me of the fact that he had a twin brother who was stillborn.

Part of the reason for writing this book is the fact that many people still do not believe Elvis is dead, but rather went into hiding to straighten out his life. It is my expressed hope that you, the reader, be you an Elvis fan or not, will enjoy the 'fictional' mystery you are about to read.

The last thing I want to do is anger any of Elvis's loyal fans. We all admire the music of the man known as the King of Rock and Roll. This was a term that Elvis didn't really care for and at several of his concerts politely admonished fans who held up signs that read, 'Elvis is King'; with the statement, "Thank you, but there is only one true King and that is the Lord Jesus Christ."

The Elvis impersonators are just that, impersonators. This fictional story deals with someone being passed to the public as the 'real deal' and not merely *impersonating* Elvis. I hope you enjoy, 'Counterfeit Elvis'.

1

West Hollywood, CA
July 7, 1965

THE DOCTOR walked slowly out of his examination room with a dour look on his face. He was met by Colonel Tom Parker, Vernon Presley, and several close friends of Elvis, known around Hollywood as the Memphis Mafia due to the way they protected him.

The doctor had agreed to see Elvis after hours due to the celebrity status of the singer/actor. Besides, no one was to know about the ailment that Elvis was dealing with; no one.

The Colonel waited for the doctor to say something but when he didn't, the Colonel begun to question him with a barrage of questions.

"So what is the diagnosis; did that accident damage my boy's voice box? I've got to know...tell me," the Colonel snapped.

The doctor took a deep breath and let it out heavily, "The blow to the larynx that he received while filming 'Jailhouse Rock' started this entire problem. His over use of his vocal chords has worsened the problem and I'm afraid if he continues to strain his voice he will eventually lose it all together; singing wise, that is."

"What are you saying? Elvis is supposed to give up singing; is that it," the Colonel snapped, his eyes flashing hot with anger?

"Yes, that is precisely what I'm saying. He's lucky his voice has held up this long. I told you about this a year ago that he needed to take a long, long rest from singing. I know that's his career, but his career could soon be over as far as singing goes; and I mean very soon," the doctor said with his own glare back at the Colonel.

The Colonel looked away, deep in thought. Elvis unable to sing! He couldn't let that happen; but what could he do to change this terrible situation. There had to be something he could do; but what?

Suddenly he raised his head as a light went off in his head and a slight smile tried to force its way on to his face.

"How long would you say we have if we continued at the present rate of movies and record albums," the Colonel asked bluntly.

The doctor looked at Parker in disbelief. He slowly shook his head and then answered.

"I'd say no more than one year; tops. If you slowed down to say half of what Elvis has been doing then you might get two, or two and one half years more out of him. But, he will start to show the effects soon if you push him."

"One year...yes, that would be plenty of time I think," the Colonel said nodding his head slowly.

The doctor shook his head also as Elvis walked out of the examination room. Elvis had a dejected look on his face as he spoke to those waiting for him.

"I can see the doctor broke the bad news to you. It looks like the gravy train is about to jump the tracks," Elvis said evenly.

"Maybe not, Elvis; you know me...I'm not about to let the gravy train get derailed by something like this. I have a few things up my sleeve besides my arms," the Colonel said wryly.

"Yeah, an arm full of watches, unless I miss my guess," Elvis said with a grin that got chuckles from his friends.

"Thank you, Doctor. Send us the bill and I'll drop a little something extra in it for your silence," the Colonel said.

"I never divulge my patient's conditions to anyone. You should know that, Colonel," the doctor said indignantly.

"It never hurts to put a little extra grease on a wheel to keep it from squeaking, though," the Colonel said. "When do you want to see my boy again?"

"I'd like to see you in about three months. If, however, your throat starts to bother you, Elvis, get in here as soon as possible," the doctor replied.

"Yes, sir; I'll do that," Elvis said and started for the door.

"Goodbye, Mr. Presley," the nurse said with a huge smile.

"Call me Elvis...That's Mr. Presley over there," Elvis said with a smile as he pointed towards his father.

Once outside the doctor's office, Elvis turned to the Colonel and asked, "So what do we do now?"

The Colonel pushed the elevator button for 'Down' and then answered, "We're going to find us a perfect look alike to take over for you, my boy. And I think I know just the right one to do that for us. Yes, I think we're going to be all right. And I think you're going to be happier than you've been in a long time in the process," the Colonel said still in a thoughtful voice.

"You mean a 'counterfeit me'," Elvis said with a frown as they got in the elevator?

"Hey, I like that...a 'counterfeit Elvis'. Yes, this is working out better than I could hope for."

"I'd like to be in on this con game of yours, Colonel. If it's illegal, I want nothing to do with it," Elvis said tightly.

"It isn't anything illegal, my boy; but it is a stroke of genius on my part, I'll have to admit. I'll explain everything to you once we get back to your place. Vernon, I'll want to speak with you before I explain my plan to Elvis," the Colonel stated.

Vernon Presley gave the Colonel a questioning look, but nodded his head yes.

"I think you might know what it is I want to talk to you about," the Colonel said and then shifted his gaze to Elvis. "Son, what you are going to hear shortly will shock you. You may feel betrayed, but in the long run you'll be the happiest guy on earth. Your father will verify what I will tell you at that time. I hope you'll take this properly; I think you will, though," the Colonel said, playing the mind game with Elvis that he seemed to enjoy doing.

Vernon Presley rode in the limousine with Elvis and the Colonel in silence. Elvis sat staring out through the dark tinted windows wondering what was going to happen to him, his career, his life now.
Vernon Presley wondered if the Colonel was going to divulge a secret that he and Elvis's mother Gladys had told him about years earlier. If that was what he was about to do, he worried about Elvis's reaction to it.
The Colonel sat deep in thought as they made the drive back to Elvis's Bel Air home. A lot would depend on finding the one man who might save the Elvis empire; a man the Colonel wasn't even sure was still alive or not.
Once the caravan arrived back at the Bel Air estate, the Colonel collard Vernon and Elvis and dragged them off to the master bedroom, where he began to share his 'plan' with them.
"Vernon, you heard the doctor say that Elvis's career is through; or it will be within a year. His singing voice will be completely gone. Because of that, I'm forced to tell Elvis the secret that I swore to both you and Gladys that I'd keep from him," the Colonel said.
Vernon frowned and cast a quick look at Elvis who was listening intently to what the Colonel was saying.

"Tom, you swore you'd never tell Elvis what we told you in strict confidence. Gladys would be turning over in her grave at the very thought of you doing it," Vernon said.

"What are you two talking about," Elvis asked with a deep frown?

The Colonel looked at Elvis and then back at Vernon, "I've got to do it. Do you want to go back to living in poverty; I don't think so. We've got to take drastic measures and they hinge on what I'm about to do."

"Would one of you tell me what you're talking about? Why would Mama be turning in her grave at what you're about to tell me," Elvis demanded to know?

Vernon thought about it for a moment and then slowly nodded in agreement. Elvis watched both men with a critical eye, but turned his full attention to the Colonel when he began to speak.

"Elvis, there is someone out there who probably not only looks exactly like you, but hopefully has your voice to boot. The only one in this room who knows this young man is your daddy, Vernon," the Colonel said and then paused.

"How would you like to meet your twin brother...Jesse Garon Presley," the Colonel asked?

Elvis didn't answer immediately but gave his father a hard stare. He looked back at the Colonel and slowly asked through tight lips, "Are you about to make some stupid, morbid joke? Because if you are...don't!"

"This is not a joke, Elvis; and this is why I wanted to tell you this with your father present.

Jesse Garon, as far as we know, is alive. What we have to do is find him," the Colonel said.

Elvis glared at his father, "Is this the truth; you're not lying about this, are you?"

Vernon looked down and shook his head no and said, "We had to give Jesse up, Elvis. You were the healthier of the two so we kept you. We just didn't have the money. It broke your mama and my hearts to do it, but we had to.

"We were assured he'd go to a good couple who would love him like their own. How could we tell you that we'd given him up like we did," Vernon said unable to look Elvis in the eye.

"Sold him, don't you mean," Elvis snapped. "I'm sure some money changed hands. Say it...you sold Jesse Garon to the highest bidder."

"Elvis, you have to understand how hard it was for your parents. It wasn't uncommon in those days; the country was still in the Depression, for god's sake. You've always wanted to know your brother...now is your chance. But first we have to find him," the Colonel cut in, and then added, "Think about it, son."

2

ELVIS came out of his bedroom an hour after Vernon and the Colonel had retreated to the family room. He was still wearing a stern look on his face, but he had been deep in thought about what he had just learned.

He looked at his father for several seconds before finally allowing a smile to crawl across his face. He slowly nodded his head and said, "I've thought it over and I can understand why you did what you did. The important thing is that I'm finally going to have my twin brother with me."

"That's right, my boy. That's why I said this whole thing could be the best thing that's ever happened to you. But we've got a lot of work ahead of us. First off, we have to find your twin and get him out here to Hollywood so you two can start learning all you can about each other. You know, who your friends are, all the things you have in common; and I mean everything from A to Z," the Colonel said with a serious scowl.

"Finding him isn't going to be easy to do. If the family named him something other than Jesse Garon, which I'm sure they did, and there're no records of him being born to mom and dad, where would a person start? It seems to me that the investigation would just run into a dead end," Elvis said, and then added.

"Another thing...anyone who knows about this will have to be sworn to secrecy. And I don't mean like you, Colonel Tom. I mean, they can't tell a soul. If it gets out what has been done, we'll all be the joke of the ages."

"I've thought of all that, my boy. That's why we've got to find him and get him out here as soon as possible so he can go to work learning to be you. Of course, we don't even know if he can sing," the Colonel said.

"Oh, he'll be able to sing," Elvis said quickly. "It's my bet he'll sing better than me. Man, I can't wait to meet him. I just hope he can be found."

"As far as what his name is at the moment, I'll take care of remedying that," the Colonel said as though he'd already thought it out.

Elvis gave the Colonel a curious look as he asked, "And how do you propose to do that...No, on second thought, I don't want to know. I'm sure I'll find out soon enough. Man, I hope we're not biting off more than we can chew."

The Colonel gave Elvis a steady stare, "Elvis, do you love your fans?"

"Of course I do; you know that," Elvis replied.

"If you lose your voice, your fans will hear no more 'new' songs by you. Now I ask you...is it fair to them? If they don't know your twin brother is standing in for you, what will it hurt? And if it does get out that he's your twin brother that would be the story of the century. Your fans would receive him with open arms and hearts...I guarantee you they would."

Elvis considered the Colonel's words and slowly nodded meditatively.

"So how do we find Jesse...or whatever my brother's name is today," Elvis asked?

"I know just the man to call on for that. He's handled several very sensitive cases for the studios over the years. Let's just hope Jesse is okay, if you know what I mean," the Colonel replied.

"Yeah, I was just thinking that too. I hope he's all right. I guess all we can do is wait and see...and pray," Elvis stated.

That evening there was a recording session for a couple of songs to go on the soundtrack that would be cut for an upcoming movie entitled, 'Tickle Me'. Elvis arrived at the recording studio around 8 pm and the recording started within ten minutes from his arrival.

Elvis had just ran through a number and wasn't happy with the way it had turned out. It wasn't unusual for him to do twenty to forty or more takes on a song if he wasn't happy with it. He started the song the second time and about half way through it, hit a terribly sour note.

A look of concern shot across his face, but he quickly covered it up with a joke. He'd made mistakes on songs before, and it hadn't worried him. This time, however, it was different. He knew where the problem lay.

"Hey, would someone get me some water. My throats a little dry and I may try and sing this song while gargling at the same time," Elvis joked.

The guys all laughed.

He got the water and drank it down. He cleared his throat several times and they started again. He managed to get through the song without his voice breaking.

He still wasn't happy with the outcome of the song, but due to the strain the song put on his voice, he said he was satisfied with it. In truth...he wasn't.

Elvis taped for only an hour and a half and called it quits. This was something else that was unusual for him. He'd been known to sing all night long. An hour and a half was more like a warm up for him.

Elvis went home and sat down on the large sofa and pondered what all was happening to him, his career, and his personal life. The truth was that Elvis was getting tired of not being able to go out in public like ordinary people. He had to do things secretively and it was wearing on him.

His thoughts drifted to Jesse Garon and he smiled involuntarily. He prayed they would be able to locate his twin brother. If they could, what a reunion it would be. Or would it?

If Jesse had never been told that he was adopted, the news that his parents had lied to him all these years would be just as hard on him as it had been on Elvis, thinking his brother was dead.

Perhaps Jesse wouldn't want anything to do with the scheme the Colonel was cooking up.

There were so many intangibles here that it would be a miracle to pull this off. If they could, however, the work of Elvis would go on, only not through him, but through the brother he thought had been stillborn. He smiled at the thought of finally being able to look his identical twin in the face. That part of the scheme excited him to no end.

Elvis thought about his mother and what she would have thought about being reunited with her 'other' son, if she were still alive. He could envision that beautiful smile of hers at the thought of seeing Jesse Garon again. He knew she would be all for this, if only for seeing the other twin boy that they had told the world was stillborn.

Thinking of his mother had a calming effect on him that seemed to whisper, 'everything is going to be all right'. That thought, however, was accompanied by a feeling of uncertainty due to his knowledge of the Colonel. He wasn't sure to what extent the 'old carnival man' might go to in making things 'work out', as he liked to say.

3

West Hollywood, CA
July 8, 1965, 2:35 pm

IT WAS just another boring day in the middle of what had been a boring week which was why I was reared back in my office chair reading the Los Angeles Times newspaper. I had found a very interesting article involving a dead body that had been discovered with the man's vital organs missing.

As I read the article a cold chill ran down my spine. Who would do something like that? What perverted mind could come up with something like this? Being a private investigator after having served on two different police forces, I thought I'd heard everything; this was different.

I had just finished reading the article when the door to my office opened and two men entered wearing dark glasses. They took a position on each side of the doorway. I looked up with a concerned look on my face just as a third man entered; he too was wearing dark glasses and smoking a cigar. The man identified himself as Colonel Tom Parker, Elvis Presley's manager.

"I take it you are Sean Weigel, is that right," he asked?

"Yes, I am. What can I do for you?"

Before he answered my question he turned to the two men in black and said, "You boys wait outside in the hall. And don't let anyone in here; ya hear."

He waited until the two men had left and then turned back towards me and said, "I want you to find someone for me. You do locate missing persons don't you?"

"I do, among other things," I came back.

The Colonel smiled slightly and sat down in the chair across from me. He looked around the office and then looked me straight in the eye.

"I want to hire you to find someone for me," Parker said seriously.

"Okay, I can do that," I said and then asked, "Who is it you want me to find?"

Parker paused for a moment as he gave me a hard stare. "I want you to find Elvis's twin brother, Jesse Garon Presley," he said very seriously.

I waited for him to say he was only joking, but his expression didn't change. When I realized he was serious I replied, "I was under the impression that he was stillborn."

"That's what Elvis's parents told everyone. The truth is that the Presley's were dirt poor and realized instantly that they wouldn't be able to afford both babies. The short version is that they gave Jesse up for adoption. They never told Elvis and he was unaware of that fact until recently," the Colonel stated matter of factly.

I was somewhat dumbfounded at hearing this along with being somewhat leery of getting involved in a case like this. My next question was why?

"Does Elvis know that you want his twin brother found? And if not, why doesn't he know?"

"Yes, Elvis knows that I want to find Jesse, and he's all right with the endeavor," the Colonel responded.

"How'd you come to know about this if it was such a big secret," I continued to question?

"The Presley's told me the truth when we got Elvis a movie contract. From what Mrs. Presley said, she wanted to get the burden off her shoulders. They asked my advice as to whether they should tell Elvis what they had done or not. I advised them not to say anything due to his career just starting to take off," Parker answered.

"What can you tell me about Jesse's whereabouts; anything?"

"Nothing at all," he answered. "That was part of the contract they signed with the doctor. He would place Jesse with a good family who would love him and care for him; the family was supposedly very well to do; at least that was what the Presley's were told. They could never make contact with the boy and would not even be told the people's name who adopted him. As far as Jesse and the rest of the world would know, he was the natural son of the couple."

I shook my head, "Then it could take me a long time to locate him. Are you sure you want to do this," I asked?

"I'm here, ain't I," the Colonel snapped?

"Yeah, you're here all right. I'd like to know one thing more before I agree to this. What is your underlying reason for finding Jesse? It has to have something to do with Elvis," I pressed?

The Colonel paused as he chose his words carefully, "Elvis is losing his voice. The doctors have checked him and gave the cause that carries some long medical term that I can't even begin to pronounce. To boil it down into simple terms, his voice box was badly bruised during the filming of 'Jailhouse Rock'.

"We told the press that the reason Elvis had to go to the hospital was that he'd lost a tooth cap and it had wound up in his lung. The truth was that in the fight scene where Elvis is supposed to get hit in the throat, he really did get hit in the throat.

"That scene he played wasn't acting; it was real. Mickey Shaughnessy actually hit Elvis in the throat by accident. He had a mark he was to stand on, but they had marked it too close to Elvis.

"Mickey felt terrible about it, but it wasn't really his fault. As far as the injury goes, the doctors say it won't be long before Elvis won't be able to hit and hold a note. This injury has worsened each time he sang. I think Jesse may be the answer."

I was stunned at his candor. "You mean you want to 'exchange' Elvis for Jesse? Is that what you're saying?"

"That's it. Let me explain something to you. Elvis is a 'gold mine'. Did you know that from the time he first came on the scene guitar sales have been going through the roof? And it's all because of him. He has changed the music industry forever and it has opened up hundreds, if not thousands of jobs for people.

"He is setting records that may never be broken. For him to lose his voice now would cost many people fortunes...and that includes me. Jesse could keep the 'money train' running for another ten, maybe fifteen years," the Colonel explained.

I exhaled heavily, "I see what you mean. I don't know that it will work, but I see what you mean." I paused, "Yes, I'll find Jesse. I guess my first stop will have to be Tupelo, Mississippi."

"That's where it all began."

"That would have been thirty years ago, so I would think there are still people around there that might know something," I said more to myself than to the Colonel.

"I would imagine," the Colonel replied.

"I just have one more question for you. Why me," I asked pointedly?

"You came highly recommended by a mutual acquaintance...Roy Fitzgerald. He told me how you had kept his name, along with your findings, out of the newspapers on the attempted blackmailing that could have ruined him," the Colonel said with a grin.

"Yes, it wasn't easy, believe me," I replied.

"Of course if this investigation should ever find its way to the newspapers I'll deny ever having met you. That is why I will pay you in cash. How much do you require as a retainer fee?"

"I'll need a hundred and fifty a day, plus expenses. I'll be flying back to Mississippi to begin my investigation, so let's say two thousand to start. I'll keep you posted as to my progress and give you a written report," I said.

"Not a written report...a verbal report. I want nothing in writing that can tie me to you. Here is twenty five hundred to start," he said and laid an envelope on my desk.

"A receipt," I asked?

He merely shook his head no as he pulled a business card from his pocket and laid it on the table.

"You can leave your progress report at this number. You will record it onto an answering device and I'll get it," he said assuredly. "Once I've listened to it, it will be erased."

With that he turned to go. It was obvious our first meeting was over. When he got to the door he looked back and smiled.

"Until we meet again, Mr. Weigel," he said, and before I could answer turned and walked out into the hall and headed for the elevator with his two bodyguards following ahead of him.

I sat there for several seconds wondering if I was doing the right thing by taking this case. One thing was for sure. This would be hard to keep from the newspapers. As soon as word got around that a private investigator was asking questions about Elvis Presley's presumed stillborn twin brother, tongues would start wagging.

I called LAX Airport and got a schedule of flights to Memphis, Tennessee and booked one for the following morning at ten a.m. Since Memphis was only around a hundred and ten miles from Tupelo, I figured I could drive it and get a lay of the land, so to speak.

I called a friend of mine in Memphis and had her book me into a hotel there in the city. I wanted to familiarize myself with Memphis before heading down to Tupelo. I'd rent a car once I got there, figuring I'd be doing a lot of traveling through Elvis's old stomping grounds.

4

Memphis, TN
July 9, 1965, 8:45 pm

THE FLIGHT into Memphis was a rough one. We hit a weather system over Amarillo and it lasted until we hit Oklahoma City. We hit another smaller system about halfway between Oklahoma City and Memphis.

My friend, Nicole Benton, was waiting for me at the Memphis airport and drove me to my hotel. We went up and talked while I unpacked a few of my things. I told her I was going to stay in Memphis for a few days before heading to Mississippi. I intentionally didn't tell her my purpose for going to Tupelo because I knew she would put two and two together and come up with 'Elvis'.

"So what is the case you're working on, Sean," Nicole asked?

"A runaway; I've been hired to find a rich guy's runaway kid. It shouldn't take me too long to locate her," I lied for the privacy of my client and my neck.

The last thing I wanted was a run in with Colonel Tom Parker and the Memphis Mafia, as they were called around Hollywood. If this leaked out I'd pretty much have to leave the LA area if I wanted to continue doing PI business.

I had figured on asking questions about Jesse under the guise of doing a biography on Elvis. If people thought I was merely trying to gather information for a book, they might not be quite so suspicious. I'd have to wait and see how that played out though.

I told Nicole I would take her to dinner and she could name the place. She took me to 'the Arcade', her favorite eating place and where Elvis would show up from time to time. He had a favorite seat in the restaurant.

We had a very enjoyable meal and the conversation naturally came around to Elvis after awhile. Nicole was a big fan of his and told me a number of things he had done there in Memphis that had been kept out of the newspapers.

Things like buying a new Cadillac for a black lady and her husband that he'd just met. Or, his taking a truck load of presents, along with turkey dinners to the poor section of Memphis at Thanksgiving and Christmas time and handing them out. It was easy to see why the man was so beloved around Memphis, not to mention the world.

I naturally led the conversation to Elvis's twin brother and was amazed and pleasantly surprised at how much Nicole knew. Of course, I knew something that she didn't know. Jesse was still alive; or at least I hoped he was, anyway.

I started us on the subject with, "Elvis had a twin brother, didn't he?"

Nicole jumped at it like a catfish at a night crawler, "Yes, Jesse Garon. He was about fifteen minutes older than Elvis. Elvis always wondered why Jesse had been stillborn and he wasn't."

"Can you imagine if there had been two Elvis's," I said, letting out some 'fishing line'.

"It may not have been the same. I don't know? I kind of like to think Elvis was a unique individual. If there were two of them I don't think the charm would have been there the way it was and still is."

"Maybe not," I said, "But if Jesse could sing like Elvis what a duo."

Nicole smiled and then changed the subject, sort of.

"You know, that reminds me of something. I had a friend tell me that she saw a man who looked so much like Elvis it was amazing," Nicole said with excitement in her voice.

"Oh, when was this," I asked, my curiosity rising?

"About six weeks ago. She said she had pulled into a service station and had gotten out to buy some gum, when this late model Cadillac pulled in and the man driving it looked so much like Elvis she thought it was him. The only difference was that his hair was a sandy color. She said she almost asked him if he was related to Elvis," Nicole said with a laugh.

"About six weeks ago you say...and right here in Memphis, huh?"

"Yes, but I don't think the man is from around here. She said his car had a Texas license plate and the frame said Houston on it," Nicole offered.

I couldn't hold back the smile. I'm here in Memphis for less than three hours and I've already been handed a lead, even if it was a small one. Now if I could just find out Nicole's friend's name so I could question her.

"You know, I've met Elvis a number of times," I lied.

"No...you really met him? I've seen him a few times, but from across the room or downtown. I didn't even have the nerve to approach him," Nicole said honestly.

"He's one of the nicest guys I've ever met. I don't like to name drop so I don't talk about it too much; but, since we're on the subject of Elvis, what the heck."

"I'll bet you see a lot of movie stars living out in LA like you do, huh," Nicole asked smilingly.

"Oh, yeah; in fact, I've even worked for the different studios from time to time. You know, checking out people who had gone to work there, things like that," I stated, this part being true.

"Who is the one celebrity you've met that you liked the best," Nicole asked wide eyed.

"I don't have a favorite one, but I can tell you this. Elvis would be at the top of the list somewhere," I said and paused. "You know, Elvis would get the biggest kick out of meeting someone who looked as much like him as you say your girlfriend told you the guy in the service station did. I'd like to talk to her. Who knows, it might even mean a trip to Hollywood to tell Elvis face to face," I pressed.

"Why go all the way to Hollywood? Why not just go out to Graceland and see him," Nicole questioned?

"Wouldn't a paid trip to Hollywood be more exciting, though? Be honest," I said with a smile.

"Yeah, I guess it would, but Graceland wouldn't be too bad either," Nicole argued.

"It might wind up being both. If Elvis likes someone they'd be welcome at Graceland, too."

"My friend's name is Julia Cunningham. I could give her a call and have her meet you for breakfast or lunch tomorrow, if you'd like," Nicole offered, and I accepted.

"That would be great. Yeah, she can take me to her favorite restaurant, too," I smiled.

Nicole and I switched subjects and talked about her plans for the future. She said she'd just broken up with a guy she'd been dating for over a year and was hoping to meet a nice guy and get married.

The evening finally came to a close when jet lag hit me and I needed to get some sleep. Nicole drove me back to the hotel and we said goodnight. I had her drop me at the front door and as we said goodnight and I watched her drive away I noticed a black sedan parked at the curb a few cars back from where Nicole had parked. The driver was watching me like a hawk.

When I held my gaze on the driver he dropped his head so quick it's a wonder he hadn't suffered whiplash. I didn't think much of it at the time, but later I would remember this.

    I went up to my room and took a shower before going to bed. The people in the room next to mine woke me up at 2:30 am yelling at one another. I could tell by their voices that alcohol had played a major role in their argument. A call to the manager quieted them down.

5

July 10, 1965
Memphis, TN 8:00 am

AFTER A RESTFUL night's sleep, once I got back to sleep, I gave Nicole's friend, Julia Cunningham, a call and found out that Nicole had already called and told her I might be getting in touch with her. We agreed to meet at a restaurant of her choosing at 10 am, because she had appointments all afternoon.

I looked in the phone book and got the address of Hertz Car Rental. There was an agency about two blocks from where I was staying so after checking out of the hotel I walked over to the rental agency. I got a white Pontiac Bonneville, drove back to the hotel and checked out. I figured I'd be leaving Memphis and if I needed to stay another night I would find another hotel.

The restaurant turned out to be just down the street from the old Sun Records Recording Studio. I met Julia there and found her to be as pleasant as Nicole. We took a table and made small talk for a few minutes. Eventually the conversation came around to Elvis and the man Julia had seen who looked so much like him.

"So this guy looked a lot like Elvis, huh," I said.

"Not a lot...exactly. If it hadn't been for his hair being a light brown, almost blonde I would have sworn it was Elvis. He must have been used to it, because he gave me one of those Elvis smiles just before he drove off," Julia said seriously.

"You don't think it was Elvis wearing a wig, do you," I asked?

"If it was Elvis, he was driving a car with a Texas license plate and a license plate frame that read Houston Cadillac on it."

"Hmm, that is interesting. That would be an interesting investigation, wouldn't it? If I wasn't trying to run down this rich kid for his family I might follow up on that," I said, hoping to throw her off my real investigation.

"Yes, it would be. I've heard that everyone has an exact double in this world and I believe it now. I have seen Elvis a number of times and believe me, these two could pass for identical twins," Julia said and then smiled.

"That's funny...Elvis had a twin who died at birth, didn't he. Well, he's got another exact look alike out there."

I looked out the window in the direction of the Sun Record building. I was thinking of the big name entertainers who'd gotten their start with Sun. There was Johnny Cash, Jerry Lee Lewis, Carl Perkins, Roy Orbison, and of course, Elvis. I started to look away when something caught my eye. It was a black sedan parked at the curb in a parking space that would give the driver a good view of the restaurant.

We had already placed our order and were waiting for it to be served, but I excused myself and walked to the front door of the restaurant. I pushed the door open and started walking towards the sedan when the driver suddenly started the engine and pulled into traffic.

I stood and watched the car go to the next corner and make a right turn. If he was going to watch us, he'd have to do it from somewhere else. The question I had was why would anyone be following me? I went back to the table just as our food arrived.

We continued to make small talk as we ate and I learned a lot about Julia. She had moved to Memphis from Chicago due to being reassigned to the Memphis area. When I asked her what her job was I got an answer that shocked me.

"Oh, I work for the FBI," she said with a smile.

"The FBI you say," my words coming out an octave higher than normal.

"I'm not an investigator, although I have gone along with one once. My job is in 'records'," Julia informed me.

"Records...so you and Elvis have a lot in common," I joked.

Julia laughed, "I'm afraid it's not that kind of records I deal with."

That might explain the black sedan today, but it looked like the same car I'd seen at the hotel the night before. I needed a little more information.

"How did you and Nicole happen to meet," I asked, truly wanting to know.

"Julia works with me. She helped train me in the use of a new filing system the Memphis office had come up with just before I arrived. We hit it off instantly."

Now I really was stunned. I didn't know that Nicole worked for the FBI. The last I'd heard she was working as a private investigator here in Memphis with a guy by the name of Philip Connelly. I hadn't asked her about her job the night before figuring she was still on the same job. It looked to me like someone was following the two women; and not me. Now the question became...why?

"I would imagine that the FBI has quite an extensive file on Elvis," I stated.

Julia pursed her lips as she thought about my question. Finally after figuring no harm could be done, she nodded her head yes.

"Almost as much as we have on Colonel Tom Parker," Julia said with a wry grin.

I didn't take that subject any further. It was time to change subjects again. I managed that by asking more questions about Julia. I learned a lot about her.

6

WE FINISHED our breakfast and said goodbye. I knew now that after my trip to Tupelo, I'd have to make a trip to Houston, Texas. That is unless I learned something in Tupelo that changed my mind.

Since it was just a little over a hundred miles to Tupelo I headed in that direction. I still had plenty of daylight and could be down there before people I would need to talk to quit work for the day.

I took Highway 78 out of Memphis. The highway passed through a number of small towns; Byhalia, Red Banks, a larger town named Holly Springs, on down through New Albany and eventually, Tupelo.

My first stop was the newspaper office. I wanted to look at an old newspaper from January 1935. It just so happened that they had a copy and I checked the births. Sure enough, there it was; the announcement of Vernon and Gladys Presley's twin boys, Jesse Garon (stillborn) and Elvis Aron.

The announcement also carried the name of the doctor who'd delivered the babies. His name was Dr. William R. Hunt. I found out from the woman who ran the records department that the doctor had long since died, since he was 68 years old when he delivered the twins.

I checked other births that had occurred that day as well. There was another baby who had been stillborn on the same day as Jesse and Elvis; that being January 8th. It didn't list a name since the mother and father had not yet decided on one. That birth took place two hours before the Presley's twin boys were born. For a name they had merely put 'Baby Boy'.

The article gave the young couple's name as Joe and Sally Duncan; the delivering doctor was Dr. William Hunt. There address was a PO Box number. That meant the post office would have records of any moves they might have made; if, that is, they had left a forwarding address.

I thanked the woman and started to leave when she stopped me with a question.

"So, did you find out what it was you were looking for," the woman in her late fifties asked?

"Somewhat," I smiled. "I'm doing a historical check on Elvis for an upcoming book I'm writing and I just wanted to pick up a little local knowledge about the man," I lied.

"I can tell you a little bit, if you didn't find out all you wanted to know in the newspaper," the woman said with a smile.

"Oh, really," I replied somewhat surprised?

"I was born here in Tupelo and knew about the Presley's, although I didn't actually know them. What would you like to know?"

"I was wondering about the birth of Elvis mainly," I said with a smile.

"Oh, well I can tell you someone to talk to about that," the woman said flashing her own smile. "You want to talk to Edna Martin. She was the midwife who helped Dr. Hunt with the deliveries," the woman said.

"Edna Martin," I said committing the name to memory. "Does she still live here in Tupelo?"

"Yes, sir, she does. Just a minute and I'll give you her address. I'm sure she'd like to talk to you about the birth of the Presley twins."

The lady scribbled down an address and handed it to me. When she saw the look on my face, she smiled and took the piece of paper from me, and on the back drew a simple map I could follow.

I thanked her profusely and went back to my car. I studied the map and once I had my bearings drove to Edna Martins' address.

Finding the address with no trouble, I got out and went up to the front door. I knocked and waited for someone to answer. When no one did, I knocked again; a little harder that time.

"Are you looking for me," a woman said, sticking her head around the corner of the house.

"If you are Edna Martin I am," I smiled.

"I am; what can I do for you, honey," she said with a Southern accent?

"I'd like to find out a little about Elvis and Jesse Presley's birth. I was told you acted as midwife for the doctor; is that right?"

"I sure did. I didn't know it would turn out to be such a famous night, but it sure did," she said as she walked up to the porch where I was standing.

"I'm writing a book on Elvis and I wanted to get some information from people who knew him before he became famous. I take it you were on staff at the hospital," I asked?

"Yes, I worked part time in the kitchen at the hospital. Sometimes Dr. Hunt would ask me to assist him with a birth. Oh, I remember that day like it happened just last week," she said.

"Oh, other than Elvis being born that day, what happened to make it such a memorable day," I pressed?

"That's the day my husband asked me to marry him. He drove an ambulance for the hospital. Naturally I said yes," she smiled.

"Naturally," I said returning her smile. "What can you tell me about Dr. William Hunt...anything?"

"He was a well liked and respected man. He cared about people. Why, he only charged the Presley's $15.00 for delivering the two babies. He gave me five dollars. He was a wonderful man."

"It sounds like it. What do you know about the young couple who also had a baby born that day? That baby, too, was stillborn. Their last name was Duncan; Joe and Sally Duncan to be exact?"

"Sally went to school with my younger sister. Everyone knew that they had to get married. She was a good girl; very kind. They still live near Tupelo. I see her every so often; you know shopping and such," she said.

My excitement rose, "You wouldn't happen to know their address would you? I'd love to talk to them and perhaps give them a mention in my book."

"I can tell you how to get to their house, but they have a PO Box number. If you take Highway 78 like you're going to Memphis, they live just out on the outskirts of Belden. It isn't far from here.

"You'll see a big red barn on the right side of the highway; it's out near the road and there's a small farmhouse settin' back a ways.

"The mailbox has the name P. T. Riggins on it, but Joe and Sally rent the place. Riggins is the owner and gets some of his mail there but makes them use a PO Box for some unknown reason. I think he's trying to fool the IRS, to be honest, because he won't let the Duncan's use that address to get their mail at," the woman said seriously.

"He probably doesn't want anyone to know he's renting the place so he won't have to pay income tax on it; is that what you think," I asked, fueling the fire of gossip.

"That's exactly what I think; thank you very much. Now, I can also tell you this, now that you've got me thinking about it. Dr. Hunt was also the doctor who delivered Sally's baby," she stated.

I'd gotten that from the birth announcements, but acted surprised at the news.

"Is that right? Dr. Hunt was a busy man that day. He delivers one baby and a few hours later he delivers the Presley twins," I said thoughtfully.

The woman looked at me quizzically and asked, "How'd you know about the time difference in deliveries?"

41

"Oh, I read it in the birth announcements in the newspaper archives. I just happened to notice it while reading about the Presley's," I said quickly covering my tracks.

"Oh…," she said and looked around to make sure there was no one within earshot. "I'll tell you something you won't find in the newspapers."

I looked around the same way she had before saying, "Oh, and what is that?"

"Dr. Hunt helped a lot of people get babies by way of adoption. See, this area was very poor and a lot of people just simply couldn't afford another mouth to feed. Especially if they all ready had a houseful of little ones running around, you see. I heard he'd arrange for an 'adoption'," she said in a whisper.

"Is that right? How would he do it without going through proper channels," I asked?

"We're talking the mid '30's. Things were a lot more lax in those days," she said and looked around again. "Take a look in those old newspapers again and notice the number of 'stillbirths' that took place."

It looked like what Gladys had told the Colonel was right. The doctor had arranged for a 'stillbirth' due to the fact the Presley's just couldn't afford two babies. The woman wasn't finished.

"Let me tell you this, though. The doctor always checked the prospective new parents out. If they weren't suitable, they didn't get the baby," she said with a head nod.

"How do you know all this," I questioned?

"As you all ready know, I worked part time at the hospital and as a midwife with the doctor. I kept my eyes and ears open and my mouth shut. If the doctor could do a good turn for someone who was I to upset the apple cart," she said with a frown.

"You don't think that's what happened to Jesse Presley, do you," I ventured?

"Jesse...no, I don't know. I'd have to say a definite 'maybe'. The Presley's didn't have much to live on, I can tell you that. The Presley's lived down in Shake Rag; that was the poorer section of town; it's a little better now. The Duncan's had even less than the Presley's."

"I don't suppose there's any records of these transactions kept anywhere, is there," I asked?

"Now, what do you think? They'd be crazy to keep a record of these transactions."

"Yeah, I can see that. Well, thank you, Edna. You have been so helpful. I don't know that I can use any of this in my book, but if I do I'll keep your name out of it, how's that," I said with a grin.

"You do and I'll hire a hit man to go get you. If you're writing a book you'd better spell my name correctly. It's Edna Martin. Who knows, that book might sell a million copies. I could become famous over night," she said proudly.

"Yeah, you just might at that," I smiled.

7

EDNA had provided me with a lot of information. More than I possibly could have hoped for. This case might not be that hard to wrap up after all. Of course, finding this look alike Julia had told me about would undoubtedly take the most time.

As I drove away from Edna's house I had a better understanding of the overall situation of the Presley's back in 1935. I'd read that they buried Jesse Garon in an unmarked grave. I had wondered about the reason for that when I read it. Now I knew. It may not have been their baby that was in the grave, but that of the Duncan's.

My next stop, after driving by to see the 'shotgun' style house where Elvis was born, was just out of Belden, about four miles from Tupelo. I found the Duncan's with no trouble, but only Sally Duncan was at home. Joe was working in the field behind the house.

I parked and got out of the car. After being greeted by two large dogs, I made my way up to the house and knocked on the door. Sally Duncan opened the door, but left the screen door closed.

"Yes, can I help you," she asked, cautiously?

"I hope so. My name is Sean Weigel and I'm doing research for a book I'm writing on the life of Elvis Presley. While I was looking over birth announcements in an old Tupelo newspaper, I saw that you had a baby on the same day Elvis was born. Like the Presley's your baby was 'stillborn'," I said showing true sadness at their misfortune.

Mrs. Duncan looked down for a moment and then looked back at me and asked, "What is it you want to know?"

"I was wondering where you gave birth to your baby; was it at home or in the hospital," I asked?

"It was at home. Dr. Hunt came to the house and delivered the baby," Sally said haltingly.

"And did he arrange for your baby to be removed from the home," I asked.

"Well of course he did. You don't think he just left Gerald there do you," Mrs. Duncan said tersely?

"I'm sorry, I didn't mean for it to come out quite that way. I notice you called the baby, 'Gerald'. On the birth announcement in the newspaper it said you had not decided on a name for the baby yet, and just had 'Baby Boy'. I take it that when the baby was buried that's the name you had put on the grave; am I right?"

"Yes. The doctor took care of all the burial arrangements and after little Gerald was buried we had a memorial service at his gravesite."

"So you didn't actually see him in the casket, then," I questioned?

Mrs. Duncan looked at me very suspiciously before asking, "What is your interest in the burial of our baby if you are working on a book about Elvis?"

"It's only for a reference in the book. If you don't want me to include it, I won't. But I think people would be interested in knowing that there were two stillborn births on the day the Presley's had Elvis and Jesse," I said apologetically.

She looked down for a moment and then said, "I will agree to it, if my husband does; but, only if I can read the part about us and little Gerald before you have the book printed."

"That would be fine. The portion on you will be very respectful, believe me," I said, feeling a little guilty about lying to her since there would be no book; not coming from me anyway.

Just then I heard the sound of a tractor approaching. I looked in the direction of the sound just as Joe Duncan rounded the corner of the house. He cast a quick glance at me and then drove the tractor over behind the barn.

Joe got off the tractor and walked to the house. He had a concerned look on his face and as he approached asked, "What's going on here?"

"Hi," I said, but before I could say anything else, Sally took over the conversation.

"Joe, this man is doing a book on Elvis and wants to include the fact that we suffered a stillborn birth of little Gerald on the same day the Presley boys were born," she said rapidly.

Joe looked at me and asked pointedly, "How much do we get out of it?"

"Well, there wouldn't be any money in it; but, it might get you some down the road. The more people that read about your misfortune might even want to do an entire book on you and your family," I said sensing that he was hoping to cash in on this.

"If there ain't no money, then there ain't no story," he snapped.

"I don't have to have your permission; I just wanted to ask you about it, that's all," I replied tightly.

"What do you mean, 'you don't have to have our permission'," Joe said angrily. "I'll sue you for a million dollars."

I could see my conversation had come to an abrupt halt, and since there was no book figured I'd gotten all I needed.

"Okay, we'll leave your name out of it. You can just go on being known locally instead of around the world," I said holding my hands up in the air.

The thought of being known around the world must have struck a chord with Joe because his tone quickly changed.

"Hey, wait a minute. I'm sorry I snapped at you. I had a tough day out yonder in the field and have no call to take it out on you. Why don't you come on in the house and we can talk," he said pleasantly.

"Okay, I'd like that," I responded.

We went in and Sally headed straight to the kitchen where she was cooking their supper. I sat down on a sofa and began to talk to Joe. I filled him in on what I knew and he added a little bit more.

"I knew Vernon Presley. We were about the same age and worked at a couple of places at the same time. He was all right. Gladys was a lot of fun. She was a very impulsive gal as I recall.

"Vernon actually contacted me after we lost our baby and told us that he knew exactly how we felt. He even offered me twenty dollars to help out with our expenses. I thought that was strange since they didn't have much more than we did," Joe said.

Just then Sally called from the kitchen, "Mr. Weigel, would you like to stay and have some vittles with us. We're having fried chicken, okra, mashed potatoes and gravy and biscuits."

I usually don't take chances eating with people whose cooking I'm unfamiliar with, but it sounded so good I said yes, I'd like to stay.

Sally was a great cook and forced me to have two helpings. She didn't have to force Joe; he ate like he had been starving. After supper she brought out a huckleberry pie and homemade ice cream.

We talked for another hour after supper and I finally told them I'd have to be going. Joe was all for being referred to in the book I 'wasn't' going to write. I hated tricking them this way, but that's part of what being a private investigator is all about. You have to be a little bit deceptive if you're going to be good at what you do.

I had been very lucky getting the information I had so quickly. Sometimes it's almost as if there's an invisible hand going ahead of you, preparing the way. This could be one of those times.

It was starting to get dark by the time I drove out of the Duncan's driveway and headed back in the direction of Memphis. As I pulled out onto Highway 78 I looked in the rearview mirror and noticed a car parked on the shoulder of the road turn its headlights on and pull out onto the highway. The car was a good hundred and fifty yards down the road from the Duncan's driveway.

I watched the car suspiciously, noticing that the driver certainly wasn't in any hurry to go around me. I held a steady speed and kept my eye on the car behind me.

As I was leaving Belden I saw a small service station and although I still had over a half tank of gas, decided to stop and fill it up. I hit the turn signal and watched the mirror to see if the car behind me did likewise. It didn't.

As I got out of the car at the Mom and Pop's gas station and grocery store I gave the car that had been tailing me a hard stare as it passed by. This car was a dark green and when the driver didn't look my way I dismissed it as just my suspicious nature.

After filling the tank with gasoline, I headed on back to Memphis to turn the car in and catch a flight to Houston. My first stop there would be Houston Cadillac. If they had a guy that looked as much like Elvis as I'd been told, he wouldn't be hard to find.

8

Memphis, Tennessee
July 10, 1965, 9:30 pm

I WAS able to return the Pontiac at the Hertz rental office at the Memphis airport. I had to wait about three hours in order to catch a flight to Dallas where I'd have to transfer to another flight on down to Houston. Before I did anything else I called the number the Colonel had given me and left my verbal report.

I went to a gift shop and picked up an LA Times newspaper to see what was happening back in Los Angeles. When I got to the second page I saw a name that was familiar to me. The name was Craig Lansford, another private eye. He'd been found shot to death in his downtown office.

I'd known Lansford when we were both hired by MGM Studios to investigate a series of accidents. We'd hit it off right away and found we had a lot in common. One thing we shared in common was a love for our work.

There weren't a lot of details to Craig's murder, but that wasn't unusual. The police always hold back certain things from the press for fear of

51

exposing certain things about the case that only the perpetrator of the crime would know.

As I was in the process of folding the paper in half to read another story, I noticed a man watching me from a seat about twenty feet away. He was wearing a suit and had a hat pulled down slightly over his eyes.

Naturally I became suspicious of the man. I cast a casual glance in his direction from time to time to see if he was actually watching me. Before long I had the feeling he was keeping an eye on me. Again I wondered why?

I figured on letting the man watch me without knowing I was onto him. If he got on the flight to Dallas with me, I'd have a pretty good idea if I was being followed or not. If he then got on the flight to Houston I'd be ninety nine percent sure he was following me.

Each time I'd turn the newspaper pages over I'd give the man a quick casual glance. I felt better about his being there when he was joined by a woman who appeared to be his wife. I smiled as I felt a sense of relief. I hate being followed when I don't know what the reason is. Then again, I hate it when I do know what the reason is.

Finally we were allowed to board the plane and were in the air within thirty minutes. The man I thought had been watching me had boarded the plane alone; the woman kissing him goodbye at the boarding zone.

He had taken a seat several rows behind me. When I looked back in his direction he had his head back and appeared to be sound asleep. If he was following me, why not; where could I go flying at thirty thousand feet?

The flight to Dallas was fairly smooth. We didn't hit any bad weather and the pilot told us that the weather in Dallas was sultry. I checked my watch and saw that it was nearing three o'clock in the morning. I decided I should catch a few winks of shuteye while I could.

The announcement that we were approaching Dallas woke me up. I love traveling this way when I can actually sleep through the trip. When I looked at the guy I thought had been following I figured he felt the same. He'd slept the entire trip.

Once the flight landed and we were allowed to disembark I found which gate I had to report to for my connecting flight. The man from Memphis walked up next to me and when I looked at him smiled.

"Are you going to Houston, too," he asked?

"Yeah, is that where you're headed," I asked?

"Uh huh; I'm a traveling salesman and my route covers a lot of territory. If you travel much through the south we'll probably run into one another again," he smiled warmly and then asked, "What is it you do?"

"I'm a private investigator," I said.

"A PI...really," he gushed? "Oh, man, that is what I've always wanted to do; but, I guess I'll always be stuck in sales. I'm good at what I do," he said and then added under his breath, "I'd better be."

We sat down in the boarding area, but only had to wait about forty minutes until we could board the plane. Another fifteen minutes and we were in the air on our way to Houston.

I sat towards the middle of the plane and the salesman sat in the back. The flight went very smooth and soon we were disembarking and heading for the luggage area.

The salesman had just grabbed his luggage off the belt when a woman walked up to him and threw her arms around him. He gave her a kiss and as they started to walk away, cast a quick glance in my direction. The raising of his eyebrows and slightly embarrassed smile told me the man must have two families he was supporting. No wonder he'd made the remark that 'he'd better be good at what he did'.

My luggage was the last one to come out of the chute. I grabbed it and headed for Hertz car rental again. I rented another car and tossed my suitcase and overnight bag in it and headed for downtown Houston.

I found a nice hotel that I'd call home for a couple of days and got checked in. Once I'd put my things away it was time for another shower. I was dog tired as I called the desk for a wake up call at 10 am. I went out like a light.

Houston, TX
July 11, 1965, 10 am

It seemed like I'd just closed my eyes and the phone by the bed rang. It was already my wake up call. I couldn't believe it. How time flies when you're truly enjoying good sleep. I'd gotten around five hours sleep.

After I'd gotten dressed I went downstairs and grabbed some breakfast in the hotel's restaurant. My waiter was a friendly guy with a ready smile. I thought he might be able to get me heading in the right direction, so I asked him if he knew where Houston Cadillac was located.

"I sure do. It's about two blocks that way," he said pointing to the north.

"Great," I said.

"So what would you like for breakfast," he asked?

"Two eggs over medium, bacon, whole wheat toast and coffee," I said giving my standard breakfast order.

"A number two," he smiled.

He left to turn my order in, but was back shortly with a pot of coffee. I thanked him and took a long look around the restaurant. I like to play a guessing game of what I envision people I see doing for a living.

I saw one man who had to be a bookkeeper due to the wire rimmed glasses he was wearing. Another man was obviously a big time businessman by the dark glasses he was wearing. Another man was...watching me very closely...until I looked in his direction that is.

My first thought was that maybe he played the same kind of guessing game that I did. As I continued to keep an eye on him, though, it suddenly dawned on me that I'd seen this man at the airport in Memphis. It was when I'd gone into the gift shop to pick up a newspaper.

It was plain to see that he didn't want to be caught waiting for a food order in case I should leave the restaurant because it appeared that he was only having coffee.

When my order arrived I took my time eating and kept casting a casual glance in the man's direction. He tried to make it appear he was ignoring me, but I knew he wasn't. He also checked his watch a lot.

Once I finished my breakfast I asked the waiter if there was a phone booth nearby. He told me there was a pay phone in the hallway that led to the restrooms. I left a five dollar bill on the table that more than paid for my breakfast and headed for the phone booth.

From the phone booth I could still see the table where the curious man was seated. I called the front desk of the hotel and asked them to page Mr. Sean Weigel. I waited in the phone booth until I heard the page.

My 'tail' looked up quickly when my name was announced and he looked towards the phone booth. He was following me all right and he knew my name. Now that I knew for sure he was following me it would be easy to lose him.

I walked out of the phone booth and headed for the front entrance to the hotel. After I passed the man's table I watched him in the large mirror that was near the front door of the hotel.

Sure enough...he got up and followed me out of the restaurant. He had to know that I'd rented a car, and he might have one already, himself. If so I'd know shortly.

I walked out onto the street and waved for a cab. A yellow taxi stopped and I jumped in the back seat and told the driver to go around the block. I tossed two dollars on the front seat and looked back at the hotel entrance.

The man following me hurried outside and waved frantically for a taxicab. As soon as my cab turned the corner I told the driver to stop and let me out. I'd already paid him, so he stopped and I jumped out and motioned him on. He drove off while I rushed to a drugstore and went inside.

Within a few seconds another cab tore past the drugstore in pursuit of the yellow cab I had been in. I had to smile at my craftiness. Okay, so it wasn't much, but it had worked.

I walked back to the hotel parking lot and got in the Ford Mustang I'd rented and made the short drive to Houston Cadillac. I was still in a quandary about who would be following me. I'd find out soon enough, I thought to myself.

I found a parking space just down the street from the Cadillac showroom and didn't have to wait long before I had a salesman walking towards me with a big smile on his face.

"So which one do you have your eye on," he asked?

I smiled as I replied, "You."

He looked funny and took on a serious look.

"Don't get nervous, I'm not a process server," I laughed.

"Whew, that's a relief," he said going along with the joke. "So how can I help you?"

"I was wondering if you would happen to know of an Elvis look alike that drives a Cadillac that he purchased from your dealership," I asked, coming right to the point.

He grinned knowingly and nodded his head slowly, "You're looking for Danny Breedlove. He looks so much like Elvis it's spooky," the salesman said.

"Danny Breedlove, you say. I take it he lives here in Houston then?"

"Yeah, he does. What do you want with Danny? He isn't in any trouble is he? We're pretty good friends and he's a very good customer," the man said.

"No, no, he isn't in any trouble. It's just that we're looking for an Elvis look alike to do some commercial work for a product. I work for Sutcliff Advertising in Los Angeles and I heard about Mr. Breedlove from a friend of mine here in Houston who had seen him a couple of times, but didn't know his name," I lied again; something that was getting a little too easy.

"I'll call him and ask him if he's interested in talking to you. If he is, then he can tell you how to find his place; if not you don't know his phone number or his address," the salesman said dropping the smile.

"That's fine with me," I said, hoping that this Breedlove guy would want to talk to me.

The salesman walked back to his office and I could see him making a call through the office window. He talked for a moment and then motioned for me to come inside.

"Danny will talk to you," he said and handed me the phone.

I took the receiver and said, "Hello, Mr. Breedlove, my name is Sean Weigel and I'd like to talk to you about doing some television commercial work for us. It could be very profitable if you meet our requirements," I said confidently.

"Oh, and what are your requirements," he asked?

"One is that you have to look like Elvis Presley; the other is that you have to sound a little bit like him," I said.

"That's it," he asked?

"Yeah, that's it. Of course you'll have to be willing to go to Los Angeles to do the commercials," I went on.

He was quiet for a moment and then asked, "Would I get to meet Elvis?"

"I'm sure that could be arranged. That is if you pass the screen test for our commercials," I said, noticing that the salesman was listening very intently.

Breedlove was quiet for a moment and then asked, "What made you come looking for me?"

"We got reports from some of our people we have here in Houston, as well as some in Memphis, that they had seen a man who looked remarkably like Elvis. That was enough to have me on a plane back here," I said.

"I see. Yeah, I guess so...why not," Breedlove said evenly.

"Where can we meet so I can get a good look at you myself," I questioned?

"I'll come to where you are. I want them to check my car out anyway," Breedlove replied. "I can be there within twenty minutes."

"I'll be here. Oh, by the way, Mr. Breedlove; can you bring a copy of your birth certificate with you. I'll need to get some pertinent information off of it," I said, hoping I didn't spook him.

"Yeah, sure; is that all I'll need to bring with me," he asked?

"That's it," I replied.

"Okay, twenty minutes," he said.

"Twenty minutes," I replied and we hung up.

9

DANNY BREEDLOVE pulled into the Houston Cadillac dealership exactly twenty minutes from the time we'd ended our conversation. I was looking out the window when he drove in and when he got out of the car I was stunned. This man did look exactly like Elvis. He even wore the same kind of flashy clothes that Elvis did.

Danny walked to the showroom and when he saw the salesman who'd called him standing alongside of me, extended his hand.

"Hello, Mr. Weigel, I'm Danny Breedlove."

"My lord, you do look like Elvis; except for the hair," I said.

"I thought about coloring it black, but thought better of it. I didn't want to live with the hysteria it would cause when I went out in public," he said.

"I can see where it would. Boy, if you and Elvis got together you could sure spread confusion around Hollywood," I said with a chuckle.

"So you think I might get to meet Elvis, huh," Breedlove said.

"I can almost guarantee it. I know he's going to want to see you," I offered.

"When is all this supposed to take place," he asked?

"As soon as we can get you out to LA," I said, figuring that once I got him out there I would simply turn him over to Colonel Parker.

"I'm as free as a bird in a tree," Danny said.

"How about tomorrow morning," I asked? "I'll make reservations for us today on the first plane out tomorrow," I answered.

"Okay, that'll give me time to pack some things for the trip," Danny said.

"Oh, yeah, of course," I said and paused before asking, "By the way, Danny; where were you born?"

"In Memphis, Tennessee," he said with a grin. "In fact, I was born the same day as Elvis."

I had struck gold so fast my head was swimming. It made me think it was too fast. No one finds a person this fast. It was almost as if everyone I'd talked to had been set in place for me to find; starting with my friend, Nicole Benton.

There's an old adage about not looking a gift horse in the mouth. The idea is that you should be thankful for the gift and accept it graciously. Besides, if you look at the gift too closely you might find it is deeply flawed.

"You know I just had a great idea. What if your mother and father came along with us? I'm sure my people in LA wouldn't mind. Besides, I'm sure they would like to be wined and dined by some Hollywood types," I said, hoping I was doing the right thing.

The truth was, I wanted to talk to the parents and what better way than to get them on a flight to

California. If I could just pick up one clue from either one of them it would help me get a better grasp of things.

I could tell that the Breedlove's must have money by the two rings that Danny was sporting. He wore a diamond ring on his third finger, right hand, and a ruby ring on the pinky finger of his left hand. Plus the Cadillac he was driving was a new one.

"My folks are dead. They were killed in an automobile accident about two years ago," Danny said sadly.

"I'm sorry to hear that. It must have been very hard for you," I said honestly.

"Yes, it was; they were wonderful people," Danny said.

"So you won't have any trouble getting away tomorrow," I asked?

"No, none whatsoever," Danny replied.

We talked a little longer and Danny gave me his phone number and I told him I'd give him a call and let him know when our flight would be leaving. I also gave him the name of my hotel and the room number, so he could also get in touch with me should the need arise. Danny hurried out to his car and I watched him drive away.

As I turned to thank the salesman for his help in locating Danny, he grinned as he said, "That's rich; the Breedlove's being offered a trip by someone who was willing to pick up the check."

I looked at him curiously and asked, "What makes you say that?"

"That family was rich with a capital 'R'," he said and then chuckled.

"Oh, and what kind of work did Mr. Breedlove do," I asked?

"He was into oil; both here in Texas and out in California. They had oil wells wherever oil is, to be exact. Danny doesn't work at anything but music," the salesman said causing me to question him.

"Is he good," I asked?

"You'd think it was Elvis singing. He changes his voice sometimes though and imitates other singers. I have seen a lot of his shows and he's a good entertainer. You'll be getting a good talent," the man said.

When he saw the look I gave him he grinned sheepishly and admitted, "I was listening at the door."

"No matter," I said. "You'll probably be hearing a lot more from Danny Breedlove, but not necessarily by that name," I said with my own grin.

"Oh yeah, Hollywood likes to change people's names, huh," he stated.

"Yeah, and sometimes it's just one step ahead of the law," I said jokingly and then wished I hadn't.

"Oh, can you give me a for instance?"

"No, not off hand...well, yes I can. Take Dean Martin for instance. That name sounds a lot better and seems to fit him better than his real name, Dino Crocetti; wouldn't you say?"

"Yeah, I guess so. What are some others," he asked?

"Leonard Sly...changed to Roy Rogers. Marion

Michael Morrison...John Wayne; or Rock Hudson, whose real name is Roy Fitzgerald" I said.

"You're right; the real names just don't sound as good as their Hollywood names."

I thanked him again and told him I had to go. He said if I was ever back in Houston to be sure and stop by the dealership. I told him I would and left.

I went back to my hotel and as I pulled into the hotel parking lot noticed a car parked across the street with a man in the driver's seat. I wondered if this guy might be following me. Time would tell.

Deciding to let the man in the car know I was back, I went through the front door of the hotel rather than the side door to the lobby area. Once inside I spotted another man who could be the one tailing me. He was seated on a sofa reading a newspaper; a dead giveaway.

I walked over to the desk and picked up my key and asked the desk clerk if anyone had left a message for me. He checked and said no, but he did know that someone had asked if I was checked in there. He had told the man yes, but refused to give him my room number.

"Do you see the man here in the lobby," I asked?

The clerk looked around and the large room and slowly shook his head no.

"What about the guy reading the newspaper, over there," I asked and motioned towards the man.

"Oh, no; he's with hotel security," the clerk smiled.

"I see. Well, thanks a lot," I said and headed for the elevator.

I pushed the button for my floor and watched the floor indicator light as it moved downward. Just then a man walked up on my right side. I looked towards him and nodded.

He nodded, but returned his gaze straight ahead. Just then another man walked up on the other side of me. He too, looked straight ahead. I had the feeling I was surrounded. When the door opened they followed me in. Inside, they stood blocking the door should I decide to bolt past them.

"What floor," the taller of the two asked?

"Four," I said with a frown.

The man pushed four and gave the other man a glance. I knew then that the two were together. When they both turned their head almost at the same time and looked at me, I knew they were working as a team.

I took a deep breath and asked, "What floor are you two going to?"

"Four," the tall man said evenly.

"I'm in room 432, what room are you in," I continued to question?

"430 and 434," the man answered, giving me a non-smiling gaze.

I really was surrounded. I quickly assessed the two men and came to a quick conclusion...mob. They had the look, both in clothes and in physical features. Both had slightly bent noses; a good indication they had been involved in fisticuffs. Another was the bulge under their coats; as in 'shoulder holsters'.

When we reached the fourth floor and the doors opened they stepped out and stood so I couldn't bolt either way, should I decide to. I walked straight out and turned to my right. My room was about five doors down on the left; of course, so were theirs.

They fell in step behind me and when I got to my door and pulled out my key and stuck it in the lock, the shorter, stockier one of the two pushed me aside and opened the door. The taller man stuck what seemed to be a gun in my back.

The taller man put his hand on my back and gave me a shove into the room. I caught my balance and spun around ready to hit the first one who made a move towards me. Instead the smaller of the two pulled a shield from his pocket and flashed his FBI identification at me. The badge identified him as Agent Ralph Mosher; he said his partner's name was Agent Arthur Cringle.

"What is this all about," I asked hotly? "You guys have been following me ever since I left Hollywood," I snapped.

"That's right, from the moment you called your friend in Memphis, Nicole Benton. What is it you wanted to talk to her about," the tall man asked?

"Nicole...why I simply asked her to make reservations for me in a hotel since she lived there," I replied.

"How long have you been associated with Miss Benton," the smaller man asked?

"Look, I'm not going to answer any of your questions until you tell me what this is all about. I've known Nicole...Miss Benton, for a number of years. If she's in some kind of trouble, I know nothing about it," I said and then added sharply. "Hey, wait a minute; she works for you guys, doesn't she?"

"She's assigned to our Memphis office, yes," the shorter man said and gave his partner a quick glance. "All we're at liberty to tell you right now is that she has been making connections with some unsavory people and we're watching her."

I cooled down slightly, "Oh, I see. To be honest, I can't help you out there. You see I'm working on a case for a client that wanted me to do some investigative work in the Memphis area, and that's the only reason I'm down here?"

"What was your business in Tupelo all about," 'Shorty' asked?

"I'm looking for a runaway kid and I learned she might have gone to Tupelo. That's what investigators do, you know. They hire out to find people. Now if you gentlemen don't mind I'd like to get to bed. I've had a long day and I need some rest," I said, close to losing my temper.

"Okay, Mr. Weigel, but we'll be watching you; you can count on it," the tall one said and they moved to the door.

"Pleasant dreams," the short one said as they opened the door and walked out.

All I could do was stand and stare angrily at the door. Slowly my blood pressure returned to normal. One good thing came out of this meeting with the FBI; at least I knew the guys following me didn't mean me any harm...I hoped.

10

MY ANGER had cooled considerably when the phone in my room rang and it was Danny Breedlove. He sounded excited about the trip and was curious as to whether I'd made flight arrangements yet, or not.

"No, I was somewhat detained from doing so. I'll call right away and make reservations for us and then call you right back," I said.

"Okay, you have my number. I'll be waiting to hear from you," Danny said.

We hung up and I thought to myself how much he sounded like Elvis even on the phone, although I'd never spoken to Elvis by phone.

I called the airport and made the reservations on a flight leaving at 8:55 am the next morning. I then called the number Danny had given me and gave him the time our flight departed. Then I called the number the Colonel had given me and let him know that I was on my way back to LA with Jesse Garon Presley; better known as Danny Breedlove.

I went to bed and had dreams about being arrested by the FBI for impersonating a famous actor whose name I had never even heard before. No matter how hard I tried I could not convince them that I was innocent. I awoke in a cold sweat.

Houston, TX
July 12, 1965, 5:30 am

I'd left a wakeup call for 5:30 am, but was already up and dressed when it came. I wanted to be at the airport early, but thought I would give the FBI agents the slip before going out there. I didn't want them seeing me leave the Houston area in the company of Danny Breedlove.

When I got downstairs I gave a quick look see around the lobby area. I didn't see either of the men who'd paid me a visit the night before. There were, however, a couple of people there who might be agents assigned to following me. I'd soon find out.

I checked out of the hotel and walked out to the rental car. I'd know soon enough if I was being followed. Sure enough, when I pulled out of the hotel parking lot and headed in the opposite direction from the airport, I saw a light green Plymouth pull out into traffic behind me.

Having been with the Santa Clarita PD for a few years; and being the crackerjack PI that I am; I figured that since two agents had visited my room there may be two cars working as a team following me.

An investigator of any kind has to have eyes in the back of their head if they are going to last long at their chosen profession. My eyes were on the rearview mirror as much as they were on the road ahead of me. That's how I knew when the green Plymouth turned off and a light grey Ford took its place.

When I saw the green Plymouth pull into traffic ahead of me several blocks later, my suspicions were confirmed. The FBI had two cars on me. Whatever Nicole Benton was involved in had to be something very important to warrant this type of surveillance on someone who had made contact with her.

Now, I was between two cars assigned to tracking my movement. I'd have to do something extreme if I was going to lose both of them. What I saw up ahead gave me the opportunity to do just that.

There was a break in traffic going the opposite way and a curbed divider strip separating traffic. Timing my move, I waited until it would be impossible for the car behind me to cut into the oncoming lane to stay on my tail; so I cut the wheel sharply and jumped the curb. I made it with no problem, but the surveillance car got cut off by oncoming traffic and hung up on the curbing, sitting crossways in the island.

With both surveillance cars off my bumper I was able to make a few turns and make sure they didn't pick my trail up again. I headed for the airport to meet with Danny Breedlove and get him out to Los Angeles.

I turned the rental car in after dropping my luggage at the unloading zone. Looking around I didn't see Danny anywhere and worried that he might have had a change of heart and decided not to show. My concerns were soon relieved, though.

Danny came to the United Airlines counter where I was waiting, wearing a cowboy hat and dark glasses. He still had a slight grin on his face as we shook hands and greeted one another. He took a deep breath and shook his head.

"So what will happen first when we get to LA," Danny asked?

"I'll introduce you to the people you'll be working with. I'm sure you'll be impressed with them," I said, not wanting to mention Col. Parker or Elvis's name.

"You said there'd be a screen test; will that be at one of the movie studios," Danny asked?

"You know, I really can't tell you that, because that is all left up to those who'll be running the show once I get you out there," I said honestly.

"Tell me the truth...could this lead to something big," Danny asked seriously?

"It could...and I mean 'really big'," I responded.

Once again I saw what had been referred to by many as 'the Elvis smile'. This time Danny even had that slight sneer that Elvis was so famous for. I had to find out what he knew about his own birth and very early years.

"So, Danny, why don't you tell me a little bit about your life up until now? You know what I mean; your likes and dislikes; where you were born and raised. You know, things like that," I started my inquiry by asking.

"Well, according to my birth certificate I was born just out of Memphis; at home. My family has told me that I was kind of sickly as a baby and suffered a lot from colic.

"My father worked at a variety of jobs until he got a job in the oil fields as a 'wildcatter' where he learned the oil business from the ground up, so to speak. He moved my mother and me to Texas in 1941 when I was six years old.

"I started out going to school in Houston, but when my father was able to buy a large piece of property between Houston and Huntsville we moved there. It wasn't long after that move that they struck oil on our property and overnight we became rich.

"I've had the best education; although my true love is music; everything from gospel to country to blues and jazz to rock and roll.

"I put together a small band and played various clubs in the Houston area and that's been about it...so far," he grinned.

"No brothers or sisters then," I queried?

"No, I'm an only child. My mother had such a hard time with my delivery that they decided not to have anymore children; they almost lost her," Danny told me.

This was all beginning to fit together like a large jigsaw puzzle. The Presley's, due to their poverty, felt they could not afford two babies; especially with one being sickly and in need of constant doctor's care.

They arrange for the Breedlove's to take one of the twin boys; the sickly one; and they raise him like their own. They even come up with an excuse for why Mrs. Breedlove could have only one child.

73

It was my guess the Breedlove's were unable to have children, thus the undocumented adoption.

Danny and I chatted until it was time to board our flight. He was very entertaining and quite intelligent. He'd gone to college, but dropped out after a year to pursue what he called, 'a mediocre music career'.

I noticed the passengers seated near us constantly staring in our direction; or should I say...in Danny's direction. Even with the hat and dark glasses he still resembled Elvis, obviously wearing a hat and dark glasses.

I'd called the Colonel the night before and left a message about our arrival. I hoped he had gotten it and would have someone to meet us at the airport. He'd gotten the message all right and a limo and driver were waiting when we got off the plane.

Los Angeles, CA
July 12, 1965, 3:05 pm

Walking into the airport from the plane I saw a man in a chauffeur's uniform holding a sign that read 'Mr. Weigel'. Danny and I walked over to the man and he smiled at me and then did a double take when he glanced at Danny.

"Mr. Weigel...Mr. Presley; is that you," the chauffeur asked?

"I'm afraid not, sir," Danny replied.

Even the Elvis manners, I thought to myself. I couldn't help but wonder what Elvis would do when he got a look at this man who I believed to be his twin brother.

"Right this way," the chauffeur said as he headed us in the direction of the luggage return.

We got our luggage and walked out to the loading zone where the limo was parked. Danny and I had carried our overnight bags and the chauffeur had lugged our two suitcases out. After stowing them in the trunk of the car, Lawrence, the chauffeur's name, opened the back door for us and we started to climb in.

Due to the dark windows in the passenger's area of the limo we had not been able to tell if there was anyone inside or not. There was...it was Colonel Tom Parker and...Elvis.

I had started to get in first and did a double take when I saw who our traveling companions were. Danny almost knocked me over when I stopped abruptly and he ran into the back of me. I quickly sat down with my mouth undoubtedly open.

Danny, too, stopped when he saw Elvis seated next to the Colonel; whom I'm not even sure Danny noticed at the time; his gaze locked on Elvis. He slowly moved inside and sat down next to me.

Elvis was wearing dark glasses also and both he and Danny slowly removed them as they continued in their stare down. No one spoke, but I could see Col. Tom's eyes flashing dollar signs as he took in his newest project.

"Hi," Elvis finally said with a hesitant grin. "I'm Elvis Presley."

"Me too...uh, I mean...I know you are," Danny said with his mouth open slightly.

"You look enough like me to be my twin brother...are you," Elvis asked softly?

"I don't think so, but who knows for sure," Danny said giving me my opportunity to speak.

"Elvis, Colonel, this is Danny Breedlove. Danny, I guess I don't have to tell you who these gentlemen are," I said.

Danny shook his head no and then gave me an inquisitive look as he asked, "These are the people who want to give me a screen test?"

I nodded yes and the Colonel took over the conversation.

"Take that hat off so we can get a good look at you, son," the Colonel said.

Danny instantly removed the Stetson and held it in his lap. The Colonel leaned across and took Danny by the chin and moved his head slightly from side to side. He wanted to get a couple good looks at Danny's profile.

"Mm hmm, mm hmm," the Colonel said as he examined Danny's face from the front and both sides. "Yes, I think this boy will do; yes, sir, he'll do just fine. Let me hear you say something, son."

Danny looked from the Colonel to me and then back at Colonel Parker, "What do you want me to say, sir?"

"What's your name," the Colonel asked?

"Danny Breedlove...," Danny said with a questioning look?

"Well, we're going to give you another name before long. How does the name Elvis Presley sound to you," the Colonel said cocking his head to one side?

"What? It sounds great, but that's..., well, that's Elvis's name," Danny said obviously flustered.

"Let me explain this, Tom," Elvis interrupted. "You see Danny, I've experienced a couple of accidental blows to my throat and they damaged my voice box. I'm gradually losing my ability to hit certain notes and hold them for very long.

"What the Colonel wants to do; and I am in agreement; is to send me into a secret retirement and have someone else take my place. The only ones who know what we are doing are those in this car right now; with the exception of my father.

"The studios don't know what we're planning; the record company doesn't know; even my closest friends don't know. It's a cruel trick to play on society, but if we're going to keep the money flowing it has to be done.

"I don't feel good about doing it, but I'd feel even worse if I saw a lot of my friends without work. We sent Mr. Weigel out to find a look alike and I'd have to say, he found someone who could be my identical twin brother," Elvis said with a smile.

Danny shook his head slowly as he contemplated what he'd just been told. I could see the doubt in his eyes and felt like he needed more reassurance.

"What about his voice, Colonel," I asked? "What if he doesn't sound exactly like Elvis."

"We can handle that in the recording studios. You can carry a tune I hope," the Colonel asked?

"Yes, sir; in fact a lot of people think I try to impersonate Elvis, but I'm actually singing in my own voice," Danny said.

"Do you know the song, 'Love Me Tender'," the Colonel asked?

"Yes," Danny answered.

"Sing it," the Colonel ordered.

Danny looked at me then at Elvis and then back to the Colonel. He began to sing and all three of us looked at one another. Elvis broke out in a huge grin.

"...all my dreams fulfill, for my darling I love you and I always will," Danny sang.

"My lord he sounds exactly like you, El," the Colonel said with a big grin. "We've found our boy."

11

FROM THE TIME the Colonel had come to see me until I had returned with Danny Breedlove, aka, Jesse Garon Presley, had been five days, counting the 8th of July as the first day. I knew there had to be some sort of divine intervention here. No one finds a person with nothing to go on but where the person was born, in five days. It's just not that way.

The Colonel was overjoyed at my success and showed me how much by giving me a flat fee of $10,000. When he saw the look on my face he smiled and said, "I figured it would cost me twenty to twenty five thousand to find Jesse. I guess you are even better than I heard you were."

They dropped me off at my car which was parked in the long term parking area. After switching my luggage from the limo to my car and saying goodbye to Danny, Elvis, and the Colonel, I headed home.

As far as I knew my job was over. I had a good paycheck and had done far more than I could have ever expected to do in such a short period of time. The truth about Danny's true identity was in the

Colonel's hands now; and frankly I was glad to be rid of the responsibility.

Little did I know that my involvement in the 'counterfeit Elvis' case, as I referred to it privately, was just getting started. That became evident after a good night's sleep and a return to my office the next day.

West Hollywood, CA
July 13, 1965, 9:00 am

I had only been back in my office long enough to go through the messages my long suffering secretary had placed on my desk. I had a message to call a prospective customer which I did immediately. Just as I was saying goodbye to the person merely wanting to know my rates, a call came in on the other line.

My secretary, Jody James, buzzed me on the intercom and said, "Sean, Colonel Tom Parker wants to talk with you on line two."

"Thanks, Jody, I've got it," I said as I prepared to punch the second button on my phone.

"Hello, Colonel, don't tell me that Danny has already split on you," I said hoping I was merely joking.

"No, no, it's nothing like that, Sean. You don't mind if I call you Sean, do you," he asked?

"No, not at all; what can I do for you?"

"I want you to go to work for us on a permanent basis. You can keep your investigation business, but give us priority over any one else who might hire your services. Will you do that," the Colonel asked seriously.

I thought about it for a moment before answering, but then stated, "It would have to be in my best interest. What kind of money are we talking here," I asked?

"Let's say two thousand a month and expenses. And, I guarantee that you will not be required every week. You impressed me so much with your finding Jesse that I want you available anytime I might need you," the Colonel stated.

"Two thousand a month and I won't be used every week," I repeated.

"Plus expenses, remember that," the Colonel corrected.

This was too good to be true. I would have a steady income, but still be able to take other cases as well. What a deal. Naturally I said yes.

"Okay, Colonel, where do I sign," I said.

"I'll have a contract drawn up and over to you office before noon tomorrow. Between now and then I have a little job I'd like for you to look into," the Colonel said which brought a small frown to my face.

"Oh, and what is that?"

"Nothing unlawful, I assure you. All I want you to do is pick up Elvis's dental records from his dentist's office," the Colonel stated.

"Oh, sure I can do that," I said agreeably. "Where is it and I will go over and pick them up right away!"

"Uh, it's a little more complicated than that, Sean," the Colonel said with a slight chuckle. "You see, we don't want anyone to know they've been taken."

This bit of information caused me to cringe.

"Oh? And why is that?"

"We want to replace Elvis's dental charts with Danny's, and we don't want anyone to know about the switch," the Colonel confided.

"I see. So you want me to break into the dentist's office tonight, then," I replied?

"That's it, my boy. I'll leave it in your hands. One of my guys will drop off the new dental charts this afternoon. If you have any questions call the number I gave you and leave a message and I'll get back to you," Colonel Tom said and hung up before I could say anything more.

I could understand them wanting to replace Elvis's dental charts with Danny's. After all, it would be hard to explain to your dentist why Danny's mouth didn't match up with Elvis's dental charts.

I'd have to take the entire file they had on Elvis if this switch was to be pulled off. I just hoped the doctor didn't have total recall on the work he'd done on Elvis. If it was one of the dentists used by the studios he might have trouble recalling his work on one celebrity seeing as how he worked on so many. One could only hope.

I wondered who they were using to make up the dental charts and records for Danny. It would have to be someone that was in on the scheme. I would imagine it was a 'special' doctor that was on the Colonel's payroll.

The rest of the morning was used to take care of some personal business I had been putting off, so I did a little running around. I had brought some clothes with me from home that needed to go to the drycleaners; I wanted to deposit the money left over from the trip to Memphis in my checking account; and stop by to see an old client who had left a message with my secretary that they wanted to talk to me.

As I headed to the cleaners I noticed a plain looking, tan Ford pull out into traffic behind me. I couldn't hold back the grin as I thought, 'Good morning FBI'. It had to be them and I was sure it was in regards to my friend Nicole Benton.

I really didn't know Nicole's background all that well. We had worked on the same police force when we both got out of the police academy, that being Santa Clarita PD. A few years after we'd met, she quit and moved to Memphis.

I'm sure the FBI had checked me out and had that bit of information. They must be following me because of Nicole meeting me at the Memphis airport and us going to dinner. At least that's what I assumed and what the two agents had told me in Houston.

I didn't try to lose the tail they had put on me because I was merely running some errands for myself. I'd have to ditch them once I headed to the dentist's office, though. I couldn't have the FBI following me while I'm involved in the commission of a crime; that being breaking and entering.

12

AFTER GOING to the bank I swung by my ex-client's place to speak with him. He had hired me to follow his wife to see if she was having an affair; she was and it was with a man who had ties to the underworld.

He told me that he was getting late night calls from someone threatening to kill him if he didn't give his wife everything she wanted. He said the police told him there was nothing they could do until the man attempted to do him harm; in this case kill him. He wanted to hire me as a bodyguard.

I told him that I was under a retainer to someone else, but recommended a friend of mine who needed work. He was a retired heavyweight boxer by the name of Reggie Rogers. Reggie had been as high as the number 10 contender before finally leaving the ring. I gave him Reggie's telephone number and told him I'd check back with him to see how things were going.

After making one more stop to fill up my car's gas tank, I went back to the office. Danny Breedlove's dental records and the dentist's name and address had been delivered while I was away.

Now came the part I hated the most; breaking into the dentist's office to switch files.

Most private detectives are called on from time to time to break the law in order to retrieve something that belongs to their client. This, however, was a little bit different. The files belonged to the dentist and I was, in a sense, actually leaving a counterfeit file.

Not much happened the rest of the day. Since my office overlooks the street below I was able to watch the plain looking, undistinguishable car parked across the street from my building. There were two men in it and I noticed one make a sandwich run around lunch time.

When I left the office and headed home I went a round about way actually passing by the dentist's office I was to break into. It was only around three miles from where I live.

My apartment accesses allowed me several ways in which I could come and go without fear of being spotted by the surveillance team. I'd had the police tailing me before, so I knew I could lose these guys when I went to the dentist's office to switch the files.

I planned on leaving my apartment at around 12:30 am, and figured it would take me no more than one hour to make the round trip. That is if things went off without a hitch.

On the way back to my apartment I parked my car on the street in full view of anyone keeping tabs on me. When I got in my apartment I called two of my closest friends and told them I needed a cover for a job I was working on.

I explained that I had a 'tail' on me and wanted to lose them for a little while. They agreed to be at my place at midnight. I told them to wear a hat and raincoat knowing they had raincoats exactly like mine. The hats really didn't matter as long as they could be pulled down across the face.

They both arrived at around 11:30 pm and I gave them a short briefing. All I wanted them to do was get in one of the cabs I would call and have it take them to my office.

Once there, they were to get out and go inside the building knowing full well that the lobby area would be open. Stay there for around ten minutes and then go back out to the cab and have it drive them back to where they had parked their cars. I gave them cab fare and threw in an extra twenty for their trouble.

At 12:10 am I called three cab companies and requested a cab pick up fares by 12:30. The three of us went down to the apartment lobby and waited for the cabs to arrive. All three cabs arrived at almost the same time.

All three of us walked out to the cabs at the same time with our heads down and our hats pulled low across our face. I didn't venture a look towards the surveillance car I had spotted earlier until I was in the cab where they couldn't see me. I was in the middle cab.

I gave the cab driver the address where I wanted to go and watched as the other two cabs pulled away from the curb. The surveillance car's headlights went on and he made a U turn in order to follow the cab they thought I might be in. They chose the wrong one.

I had the driver drop me one block from the dentist's office and told him to wait for me. On my way to the building I slipped on my gloves so as not to leave my fingerprints all over the office.

Upon arriving at the building I went around back and was able to pick the service door lock with no trouble. Fortunately I didn't have to deal with an alarm system.

I didn't want to take the elevator in case there was a security guard on duty who might notice that one of the cars was in use. Since Dr. Early's office was on the third floor I took the stairs and moved as quickly and silently as I could.

I checked the halls for surveillance cameras, but saw none. This was going to be easy; I hoped. I found the dentist's office and noticed a light inside. Figuring it to be a night light of some kind, but not wanting to take the chance I might be wrong, I tried the door. It was unlocked.

Opening the door just a crack I could see that the light was that of a flashlight. Someone was in the office and it wasn't the cleaning crew. I doubted that the doctor would come to his office and use a flashlight, so this was someone who had probably picked the lock like I had planned on doing.

There was no need for me to confront the person, or persons inside, so I moved back down the hall to the stairwell. All I could do now was to wait until the ones doing the snooping got what they wanted and were gone.

I didn't have to wait long. Within a minute and a half two men came out of the dentist's office and one of them was carrying a file folder. What was going on here, I thought to myself? Surely someone else wasn't picking up Elvis's file? If so, what was I doing here?

The two men headed down the hallway in my direction, so I hurried up the stairs towards the fourth floor. I knelt down at a spot where I could see them as they came out, but could easily keep them from seeing me.

The door opened and the first man entered the stairwell. In the dim light of the stairwell I was able to recognize him; I had seen him several times on the movie lots I'd been on when working for one of the studios; I'd seen him, but I didn't know his name. I thought he was a stunt man, but could have been mistaken. The second man was unknown to me.

They hurried down the stairs towards the first floor. I waited until I knew they were gone and hurried back to the third floor door. Now to see if Elvis's files had been the one's they had taken. If they were I was off this case as of right then.

The door to the dentist's office was still unlocked, so I entered quickly. I saw a small lamp on the receptionist's desk and switched it on. I turned the lamp shade towards the file cabinet and saw that the middle drawer of the cabinet was ajar.

I went to the cabinet and looked at the first file folder; it belonged to someone named Murphy. That's when I noticed the gap in the hanging files in the section marked 'P'. My heart got that sinking feeling.

I checked the file at the front of the vacant area and found the name Plaugher; the one behind the open area was Proctor. The one missing had to be Presley, because there was no file with Elvis's name on it.

Something was going on here and I didn't like it. Colonel Tom Parker would have a lot of explaining to do or get a new nose job to repair the one I would break in several places. If someone is going to mess with me they'd better be prepared to go all the way; because I will.

I placed Danny Breedlove's files in the vacant area and shut the file cabinet door. As I turned to go I noticed the doctor's operating room door was slightly open. Out of curiosity I pushed it open a little further and peeked in.

At first I didn't see the doctor lying on the floor because he was behind the patient's hydraulic chair. With just the spear of light that pierced the darkened room I saw that he was lying face down. His head had been smashed with a hard object and he wasn't moving. I felt for a pulse, but found none.

I hurried back to the receptionist's desk and switched off the light. All I wanted to do then was get out of here as quickly as possible. I opened the door and glanced down the hallway. Just as I did I noticed the arrow above the elevator car light up; it was pointing up. Someone was on their way up from either the first or second floor.

I ran to the stairwell door and started down the stairs. I'd only gone about half way to the second floor when I heard the sound of footsteps that were coming up the stairs. It was my guess that someone had alerted the police; but who, and why?

I turned and hurried on tiptoes back up the stairs and on up to the fourth floor. If it was the police and they had been called here they would be going to the third floor. Listening for any sound that would clue me in on who was coming up the stairs I waited.

Within a minute I heard whispers as the policemen neared the third floor doorway. It was time for me to go a little higher in the building. If they were going to find me, it was going to be as far away from the dentist's office as possible.

The building was a seven story building, so my best bet was the seventh floor. I wasn't even breathing hard when I reached the top floor, but now what, I thought?

I had to think of some sort of cover and quick. Once the police found that body they would seal off the entire building. What I had thought would be an easy ten minute job suddenly had 'life' written all over it. I ran along the hallway checking doors to see if any of them had been left unlocked. At the end of the hall I found something that might get me out of this mess; a janitorial storage room.

The door was unlocked so I opened it and looked inside the room. There was a mop and bucket and white coveralls along with a ball cap hanging on a peg. I quickly got into the coveralls and exchanged my hat for the cap.

Fortunately there was a sink in the room so I filled the bucket with clear water and pushed the bucket down the hall to the first room I came to; an attorney's office. I picked the lock on that door and went inside.

Turning on all the lights in the room I noticed that the waste baskets were all empty, indicating that the room had already been cleaned. I remedied that quickly enough.

I rushed back to the storage room and grabbed the canvas bag used to put the trash in to take down to the huge dumpster outside. Then pushing it back to the attorney's office I went to a Xerox machine and found a ream of paper in a compartment under it.

Tearing the wrapping off the bond paper I began crumpling papers and tossing them in various waste baskets around the office. If this little scheme didn't work I didn't know what I'd do.

13

I KNEW I had a little time before the police arrived, so I went to the office next to the attorney's and picked the lock there. Looking inside I found it had already been cleaned as well. I had been right; the cleaning service had already gone through this floor, and probably the entire building. Usually they start on the ground floor; I thought...hopefully.

There were eight offices on the floor; four on each side of the hall. I picked the locks on two more offices and turned the lights on inside each one. It would make it appear that I was just finishing up my cleaning chores.

In one of the offices I found a transistor radio with an ear plug, so I grabbed it and stuck it in the coverall's pocket and stuck the ear piece in my ear. I didn't turn the radio on, so I could hear the approaching policemen.

The moment I saw the arrow over the elevator car go on I rushed back to the office where I had left the mop and bucket. I plugged the earpiece into my ear and found the radio was tuned to an 'oldies but goodies' station. I began to mop and 'bop' if you know what I mean.

The song playing on the radio was one I knew by heart, so when the police entered the brightly lit room I was 'cleaning', they found me singing gaily along with the music while mopping an already clean floor.

When the two officers entered the room I pretended to be shocked at their presence. I pulled the plug from my ear and looked at them as though I'd seen a ghost.

"What you doing up here," I asked quickly?

The policemen looked around the room quickly and then asked, "Are you the only one up here?"

"Yes, I am. My helper went home sick. What is it you're looking for," I continued to ask worriedly?

"You haven't seen anyone else in the building tonight," the taller policeman asked as I stared at the pistol in his hand.

"No, sir; nobody but Eugene...my helper," I said with a slight Southern accent.

"When you cleaned the third floor did you see the doctor down there," the second officer asked?

"Which one, there's four doctor's offices down there," I said hoping I had counted right when on that floor?

"Dr. Early, Dennis Early," the tall policeman snapped.

"Oh, he's a dentist. Yes, I saw the good doctor and the two men who came in to talk to him," I lied.

"You saw two men talking to the doctor," both officers asked at the same time?

"Yes, I was just finishing cleaning his office when the two men came in. I was going and they were coming," I said confidently.

"Can you give us a description of the men," the shorter man asked?

"Well, one was about your size and the other was about his size," I said pointing at the two officers.

"Were they white or Black, or Asian, maybe Hispanic," the shorter one asked?

"Oh, they were white...I'm pretty sure," I said thoughtfully.

"What is your name? We'll want to question you more," the tall policeman asked?

"Ray Dandridge," I responded quickly, using the name that was on a phony driver's license I carry just for situations like this.

"When was it you did the 3rd floor," the tall man asked?

"Let's see, it was just after I did the second floor and I was there at around ten thirty five...no, ten forty," I said ponderously. "I'd say it was around eleven ten or fifteen...maybe twenty."

I then asked, "What do you want to know all this for, if you don't mind my asking?"

"Dr. Early was killed sometime tonight. It must have been after you finished cleaning his office," the short officer stated.

"Oh, my Gosh, Dr. Early killed? That's terrible. He was a mighty fine gentleman from what I knew about him. What's this world coming too," I said and then opened my eyes wide as I said, "Why...I could have been killed too.

"This is upsetting. I feel a little bit nauseous. Do you mind if I sit down," I asked, feigning illness?

95

"No, have a seat over there by the door. We'll need to get a little more information from you," the tall officer said and then looked closely at me. "Are you sure you're all right," he asked?

"Yes, I just need to sit down for a minute."

I paused before asking, "This is my last office and I just finished with it; would it be all right if I go home?"

"Yeah, just give me your home phone and address and we'll be getting in touch with you," the short officer said. "We'll need some identification."

"Yes, sure," I replied and unbuttoned the coveralls so I could reach my wallet.

I pulled out my phony driver's license and showed it to the policeman. I then proceeded to write down the address that appeared on the license. If they ran a check on it they would find an abandoned apartment building. At least the building was there the last time I'd driven by it.

One of the policemen walked over to the door and looked towards the elevator. He turned and called to his partner and asked him if he'd called the murder in to homicide yet?

"No, I haven't. I thought Norman and Hooks were going to call it in," was the reply.

"Well, we'd better check. I'll go down and see if they have. You take care of things up here. Oh, and you can go since we've got your name, address, and phone number," the policeman said to me.

"Yes, sir; thank you," I said as I got the mop and bucket and set them inside the mobile canvas waste container.

I wanted out of their before they changed their minds, but wanted to look responsible enough to be convincing that I was in charge of cleaning up the offices. Once I stowed the stuff in the custodial closet and slipped out of the coveralls, I made a mad dash for the elevator.

I took the elevator down to the ground floor and when the door opened found myself staring into the face of a security guard. He gave me a curious look as to ask, "Who are you and what are you doing here?"

"The officers upstairs would like a word with you," I said.

"Oh, what floor?"

"What floor do you think? The one with the dead body of course," I snapped.

He rushed into the elevator and pushed the button while I stood there giving him the 'evil eye'. Once the doors closed I rushed out the back door and back to where the taxi cab was still waiting for me.

"You've got over fifteen dollars on this meter, buddy," the driver said.

"Just take me back to where you picked me up and I'll settle up there. You did an excellent job, and I'll let the cab company know it," I said, relieved to be out of the building that now had other emergency vehicles pulling up in front of it.

As we passed by the building the driver asked, "I wonder what happened in there."

"No telling; probably a breakin of some kind," I said and acted uninterested.

14

WHEN I got back to my apartment building I had the driver drop me at the front door. I tossed him a twenty dollar bill and a five and told him to keep the change. He grinned and said, "Anytime, sport."

I glanced in the direction of the unmarked surveillance car and saw only one man in it. He was seated behind the wheel. I figured the second man was in the back seat catching a few 'Z's'.

Once inside my apartment I dialed the number the Colonel had given me to leave messages for him. I left him a message all right; one that bordered on an obscene phone call. I knew I would get a call before long and maybe even my 'walking papers'.

I was so wound up I didn't even go to bed until a little after 3 am. Sleep finally managed to take over and I slept until the phone woke me up shortly after 7 am. It was the Colonel.

"Well, did you make the transfer," he asked?

"Didn't you get my message," I snapped back?

"I got a jumbled mess of obscenities, if that's the message you're talking about," he replied. "Did you make the switch?"

"I put Danny's dental records in the hole left where Elvis's dental records should have been, if that's what *you're* talking about," I shot back.

There was a pause on the other end before the Colonel said haltingly, "What do you mean by the 'hole' being where Elvis's records were supposed to be?"

"Look, Colonel, I don't know what's going on here, but someone killed the dentist last night and took Elvis's dental records with them. I showed up just as the two men were leaving. They had to have been the ones who took Elvis's files. What I want to know is why; and how many people knew about this switch."

"I can assure you I told no one other than Elvis and his dad about it and I know neither of them would tell anyone. Why would anyone want to kill Dr. Early," the Colonel questioned?

"Why would any one want Elvis's dental records to the point of killing Dr. Early is the question? I figure the doctor walked in on the guys going through his files and they killed him. You show me who knows about this switch and I'll show you the killers, or those in back of it, anyway," I said my anger cooling down some.

"Yes, I see what you mean," the Colonel said thoughtfully.

"I would imagine that you are going to get a blackmail note before too long. If they have Elvis's dental records because they know of what you're planning, they'll be holding you up, you can count on it," I warned.

"I don't think so; not if they were responsible for killing the doctor. They'd be putting a noose around their own necks, don't you think," the Colonel corrected.

"Yes, but they can also say that you or Elvis paid them to get the records. They would merely play dumb to Danny Breedlove's records being in the dentist's files, and they'd be believable because they don't know his are in there," I countered.

"Once Danny's are in there and he's ready to step into Elvis's shoes, the dental records they have become obsolete. Any checking of Elvis's dental records will match perfectly with Danny's," the Colonel fired back.

He had me there. The whole thing hinged on how soon the blackmail notes started arriving, if they did. If Danny wasn't ready to step into Elvis's shoes, the dental records I'd put in the file cabinet could actually work against us.

It wasn't going to be an easy task of bringing Danny up to speed on taking over Elvis's life. It all depended on Danny's (Jesse's) ability to learn all the ins and outs that had become second nature to Elvis.

Danny would have to learn the names and faces of people in the recording and movie business who knew Elvis personally. He'd have to be brought up to snuff on things about his co-stars; especially those with whom Elvis had been intimate.

There was a span of some thirty years that he'd have to catch up on. I figured the Colonel would have him studying day and night to bring this thing off. Even if it didn't work, the sensationalism of the scheme would make newspaper headlines around the world.

"So you have no idea who might have learned about the switching of Elvis and Danny," I asked?

"No I don't and that can be your first assignment as our personal private investigator. Find the ones responsible for this...and fast," the Colonel said, sounding almost like a threat.

"Okay, I will; at least I got a good look at the men's faces," I said.

There was a long pause before the Colonel said, "Oh, you did?"

His pause made me decide to keep the fact that one of the men might work at one of the movie studios. If the Colonel was somehow involved in this taking of Elvis's files by these two, I didn't want to let him in on everything I might find out about them. Why alert them that I was on to them?

"I'll keep you posted," I said.

"What about the men; could you identify either of them," the Colonel probed?

"I got a good look at their faces, but I didn't know either of them. If I see them again I'll recognize them with no trouble," I said playing him a little bit more.

"Well, let me know the minute you have a positive ID of the men. I'll handle things from that point on," he said, sounding like the controlling manager he had been of Elvis's career.

"Okay," I said and then added, "Leave my name at the front gates of MGM, Universal and Paramount so I can get in and out of them without any hassle, would you? And I'd like to get on the lots today," I said firmly.

"Yes, I'll take care of that as soon as we hang up. Like I said, though, you be sure and let me know anything you find out," Col. Tom said.

"Yeah, I'll do that. I'll talk to you later," I said and hung up.

First thing in line for that morning was to make a visit to a couple of movie lots and check some profile shots of the stuntmen that worked for them. I felt positive I'd recognize both men again should I see them.

My first stop was the MGM studio. I gave the guard on the front gate my name and he told me to go on through. It looked like the Colonel had come through on at least one lot.

I drove to the personnel office and started my investigation there. They had photographs of all their stuntmen and women. Of course I looked at the women's photos too; you know, just in case they were involved in the case somehow. Besides, one or two of them might find me attractive enough to want to cook me a home cooked dinner.

I had almost gone through all the file folders when I ran across a familiar face. It wasn't one of the men I'd seen the night before, however, it was one of the FBI agents who had paid me a visit in my Houston hotel room. His name wasn't Arthur Mosher; however, it was Rex Stoddard.

That told me something; the FBI weren't following Nicole at all. This was all about Elvis. Something was terribly wrong here. This would take some sorting out and fast.

I asked the personnel file clerk if she knew where I might find this Rex Stoddard and she told me it would take a minute for her to locate where he was working. She went into another room and was gone for around four minutes. When she came back she wrote a stage door number down and handed it to me.

"Just ask anyone outside and they can tell you where this building is. Mr. Stoddard is working as a stand-in as well as stuntman for Robert Wagner. If the light on the outside of the building is red, please do not go in. Wait until it goes out and then it will be safe to enter," the woman said polite, but firm voice.

I left and began looking for the building with that number on it. It didn't take me long to find it and fortunately the light was not red when I got there. I went in and made way to the only area that was shooting a film.

Standing behind the cast and crewmembers, I searched for this man Stoddard. He wasn't one of the men I'd seen leaving the dentist's office the night before, but that didn't mean he couldn't be involved in the murder. Only time would tell that.

As I watched the scene being shot, Stoddard suddenly moved into my view. He was getting ready to take Robert Wagner's place in a fight scene. He switched places with Wagner and waited for the action call.

"Action," the director called out and the fight began. These two stunt men were good. The fight looked so real you'd swear they were really slugging it out. Suddenly as the two men moved apart

Stoddard grabbed the back of his neck and stiffened...just before he crumpled to the floor.

"Cut," the director yelled and then asked, "What's the matter with you? You weren't supposed to fall down."

Everyone looked on and waited for Stoddard to get up and give a reason for doing what he'd done. He didn't move; he just lay there. The other stuntman moved over to where he was and knelt down beside him. He picked up Stoddard's hand and felt his pulse.

The stuntman looked at the director with wide eyes and said, "He's dead."

15

I PUSHED my way through the throng of actors, crewmembers, directors and others on the set and identified myself as a private investigator. I wanted to check Stoddard's body before anyone else got close to him.

"Don't move him," someone said as I moved up next to Stoddard's lifeless body.

I cast a quick hard glance at the person as I checked Stoddard's neck since that was what I'd seen him grab just before collapsing. I didn't see anything, but when I pulled my hand away there was blood on my fingertips.

I moved his head just enough to see where the blood was coming from and spotted a tiny hole where something had struck him and then either fell out or had been removed.

Quickly I looked around for the stuntman who had first checked Stoddard's body. He was standing next to the female star of the movie, Joan Blackman.

"Come here," I called to the stuntman.

He moved over to where I was and I stood up and looked him straight in the eyes as I asked him,

"Did you remove anything from his neck when you checked his pulse?"

"No, I merely raised his hand up so I could check for a pulse," he said seriously.

Since Stoddard had grabbed his neck when the object hit him, he must have knocked whatever it was loose. I quickly told the crowd to move away from the body.

"I want you all to move back away from the body. This is a crime scene because this man was murdered," I said, triggering a gasp from the crowd.

"What do you mean, 'murdered'," a tall, grey haired, distinguished looking men in a Brooks Brothers suit asked hotly?

"Murdered...you do know what that means don't you," I snapped and then asked? "Who are you?

"I'm Howard Kingman; I'm the producer on this movie. How do you know he was murdered," he asked?

"Something caused this man to grab for his neck. When I moved his head a second ago there was a small drop of blood on my fingertip. Whatever struck him must have been laced with poison," I said, triggering another response from the crowd; I had no idea why my statement caused their response.

"Poison...you've got to be kidding," Kingman said with a deep frown?

"No, I'm not. Why? What is it I said that caused the stir from the crowd," I questioned.

"The name of the move is ... 'The Poison Pen'," Kingman said and then looked off to his right.

"Sid, come here," he called to a short, balding man.

The man named Sid hurried over to Kingman's side and the two began whispering in soft voices. I couldn't make out what was being said, but felt it was something to do with the hype that would surround the movie once this story hit the newspapers.

I knelt down next to Stoddard's body again and began searching for the object that I believed must have caused his death. Whatever it was that had killed him, had to have been potent enough to have worked as fast as it had.

Gently raising Stoddard's right shoulder I found what I was looking for; it was a small, dart like object. It was about the size of a sewing needle and had stuck in the suit coat that Stoddard was wearing. He must have knocked it loose when he grabbed his neck and then fell on it, thus having it stick in his coat.

I was amazed at how fast the police arrived. I couldn't help but think that it was because of the importance of the movie industry, not only in Hollywood, but around the world.

The homicide detective in charge was an old acquaintance of mine. We'd never quite seen eye to eye on anything. If I said the sun came up in the East he'd saw it came up in the West.

"What happened," Detective Lou Skidmore said when he walked up and looked down at the body.

"Someone killed him," I said.

Skidmore looked from the body to the person who'd answered him; that being me.

"Oh crap; what are you doing here Weigel," Skidmore asked with a frown?

"Finding stiff's to keep you working," I snapped and then told him the truth, "I was here to talk to this man. His name is Rex Stoddard; he's a stuntman."

"What did you want to see him about," Skidmore asked me?

"That's between my client, me, and the fly on the wall," I said with a negative shake of my head.

"Oh, yeah, the private gumshoe stock answer...I know all about it. Who's the person in charge around here," Skidmore asked, looking past me.

"I guess that would be me," Kingman said and stepped forward.

"And who are you," Skidmore asked?

"Howard Kingman; I'm the producer on the movie we're shooting here."

"Tell me what happened; what did you see," Skidmore said, giving me a quick glance.

"We were shooting a scene where Rex, the man on the floor, was standing in for Mr. Bob Wagner there, when he suddenly fell to the floor," Kingman said, failing to tell exactly what happened.

"That's it? He just fell to the floor and died," Skidmore said with a frown?

"There was a little more to it than that, Lou," I interjected.

Skidmore looked at me holding onto the frown and asked disgustedly, "Okay, Weigel, why don't you tell me what 'you' saw."

"Stoddard was busy shooting the scene when he suddenly slapped his neck and within a couple of seconds crumpled to the floor. It was obvious that whatever hit his neck hurt by the expression on his face. Then, like Mr. Kingman said, he crumpled to the floor," I stated.

Skidmore started to kneel down and check the body and I added, "The object that hit him is sticking in the right shoulder of his coat."

"You moved the body," Skidmore cracked?

"Just enough to see what was used to kill him," I replied.

"How do you know that's what killed him," Skidmore asked, almost angrily?

"Well he wasn't run over by a truck, now, was he," I snapped. "He grabbed his neck and died, and there's a small dart like thing that caused it. When I put my hand behind his head I got a drop of blood on my finger; now, you tell me what you think, flatfoot. Check it out," I fired back at him.

"Where is this thing at," Skidmore said in a much softer tone of voice?

"It's stuck in his coat; his right shoulder; in the back," I said as I looked in the direction that Stoddard had been looking just before he grabbed at his neck.

I couldn't remember all the people who had been standing behind Stoddard, but I did recall there weren't very many. One was a tall thin guy who was now standing a good thirty feet away from where he had originally been. Another was a young, heavy set woman who had been standing next to the man...and was still standing next to him.

The man was looking at me and when my eyes locked onto him, he said something to the woman and they headed for one of the exits.

"Hey, you...wait a minute," I called out.

My words caused them to quicken their pace; making it obvious they did not want to be questioned. I called out, "Someone stop those two."

As one of the set builders moved to stop them, the man shoved him to the side and both he and the woman broke into a dead run for the exit door.

"Grab them," I yelled again.

By this time Lt. Skidmore had gotten in on the action. He started running after them, as I did. We were a good thirty to forty feet behind the couple when they burst through the exit door and out onto the street.

"Who are they," Skidmore called to me?

"They were standing behind the victim when he was hit," I answered.

Skidmore stopped and glared at me, "You mean that's it? They were standing behind the guy?"

I didn't wait to answer his stupid questions, but kept giving chase to the fleeing couple. I'd always said Skidmore was stupid, lazy, and out of shape, and this proved it. Well, the lazy and out of shape part anyway. His legs just couldn't function properly for very long while carrying around two hundred fifty plus pounds of fat on a five foot ten inch frame.

When I hit the street, I looked to my right and then to my left. The couple had commandeered a golf cart and was heading towards the front gate. I gave chase doing my best impression of football player Jim Brown. The cart was faster than me, though.

When I ran completely out of wind I stopped, stood bent over with my hands resting on my knees, and watched the couple stop the golf cart at the main gate, jump out and run past the guard, on their way to who knows where.

I was soon joined by Skidmore who was more out of breath than I was; and that's saying something. He huffed and puffed, "Did you get a good look at them?"

I replied, "Yeah, I can identify their backsides anywhere."

"Funny...very...funny," Skidmore panted.

We went back inside to the movie set and Skidmore questioned everyone that had been present and had witnessed the real death scene. I pulled Robert Wagner and Joan Blackman off to one side and asked them about the man and woman I'd given chase to.

"I don't know their names, but I can tell you they are both excellent at what they do. I've worked on three pictures with them," Wagner said.

"They worked on 'Blue Hawaii' with Elvis and me," Miss Blackman stated. "They are hard workers, but the man gave me the creeps from day one," Miss Blackman added.

Wagner then said, "You can get their files from Personnel, I'm sure."

I was just about to ask another question when Skidmore snapped loudly, "Weigel, I'll do the questioning, if you don't mind. I'm the police here, not you."

When he said he was the police I got the strangest look from the two actors I had been questioning. They looked at one another and Wagner stated, "I thought you said you were with the police?"

"No, I didn't say I was; you did," I replied.

"We assumed you were with the police," Miss Blackman said with a slight frown.

"When Stoddard keeled over I ran up to him and stated loudly, 'I'm a private investigator'; didn't you hear me?"

The two of them gave me another hard stare and then turned and walked in the direction of Skidmore.

"I'm a better cop than he is," I called after them, "and in better shape."

16

NO ONE who had witnessed Stoddard's collapse seemed to know the couple's names, so I headed for the Personnel office. I found the couple's photographs with no trouble and it gave a home address of 4384 Wilshire Blvd. in West Hollywood. It also gave a phone number which I jotted down along with their address.

For some reason I didn't think the information on the place where they 'hung their hats' was on the level. Why would they allow themselves to be identified at the scene of the crime when they had their names, address, and phone number just waiting for the cops to find in the personnel files? But something had caused them to bolt from the movie set. If they weren't guilty, what scared them?

Stoddard's murder left me at a 'dead end' as far as the phony FBI act went. If I couldn't find the other guy, I'd just have to wait and see what their reason was for tailing me to Memphis and then to Houston. Maybe they were 'wanna be' FBI agents; who knows?

I left the studio and headed for my favorite 'watering hole'; a small club on the outskirts of

West Hollywood called, Juno's. I liked it because it was quiet and I could do some thinking without being interrupted.

I parked my car in their parking lot and got out. I checked my watch and realized it was almost noon. I'd timed it just right. They had the best Philly Cheese Steak sandwiches in the state. I could kill two birds with one stone; lunch and a cocktail.

I walked into the dimly lit lounge and noticed my favorite booth was occupied by two women. I saw my second favorite booth, the one next to it, wasn't, so I headed towards it. Just as I reached it, someone called my name.

"Sean, would you care to join us," a feminine voice said.

I turned and found myself staring into the face of Ann-Margret. She wasn't the one who had called my name, though; it was the other woman seated with her...Juliet Prowse.

I'd been hired by Frank Sinatra at one time to act as a bodyguard for Miss Prowse when she had thought someone was following her. She and Frank had a thing going for a short period and he was worried about her.

"Well, hello there," I said as I did a double take. "Yes, I'd love to join you. What brings two high class ladies such as your selves to a dive where I'd be hanging out," I asked trying to sound clever as I sat down next to Juliet?

They both laughed at my quip, so I guess I pulled the 'clever' part off okay. Either that or they were laughing 'at' me instead of 'with' me.

Juliet smiled at me and then looked at her friend, "Ann-Margret, this is Sean Weigel, the private investigator I told you about; the one who stopped 'you know who' from following me everywhere I went."

"Hello Mr. Weigel, it's nice to make your acquaintance," Ann-Margret said in that oh so sexy voice of hers.

"I've been a big fan of yours since the first time I laid eyes on you, Miss Margret," I said with a smile so big it almost hurt.

"Call me Ann-Margret, please. That's what my mama calls me," the beautiful actress said politely.

"That's right...I did read that somewhere, if my memory serves me correctly," I replied.

"Oh, I'm sure you have. They have written just about everything they could about not only me, but Juliet as well. Whether it was true or not," she smiled.

Two beautiful women and me; oh the life of a private eye, I thought to myself. Just then the waiter brought their orders to them and wouldn't you know it, they had both ordered salads. I guess that's the way they keep those terrific shapes of theirs.

I placed my order and toned it down from what I normally ordered. After all, I wanted to make a good impression. While they daintily ate, I did a little people watching.

"Oh, there's John Wayne," I said as a big man and a woman entered the lounge. "And he's with Maureen O'Hara."

"They're the best of friends," Ann-Margret said.

"Speaking of friends, aren't you both friends of Elvis Presley's," I asked nonchalantly?

"Yes, Elvis and I met when we made 'GI Blues'," Juliet replied.

"And I met Elvis when we filmed 'Viva Las Vegas'; I'd say we're a little more than just friends, however," Ann-Margret said with that beautiful smile. She then asked, "Have you met Elvis?"

"Actually I have. And I must say he is a very personable and charming guy. I can see why women fall for him," I said honestly. "I'm sure you both know that he had a twin brother who died at birth."

"Yes, Elvis feels deeply about the fact that he lived and his brother didn't," Ann-Margret said.

"That would be something, wouldn't it...two Elvis's on the same stage," I commented.

"I don't know that the world would be ready for that," Juliet laughed.

"When did you meet Elvis, Mr. Weigel," Ann-Margret asked?

"Just recently," I said, not wanting to divulge too much information. "We ran into one another at the airport. I'd met Colonel Parker earlier and the Colonel was with Elvis and they gave me a ride in their limo out to where my car was parked in long term parking," I said truthfully.

"How much did the Colonel charge you," Juliet said casting a quick grin towards Ann-Margret?

"Nothing...and from what I hear that was a first," I replied getting a chuckle from both women.

Ann-Margret suddenly turned serious as she cocked her head to one side as though having a thought. She then asked me a question that caught me completely off guard.

"Mr. Weigel, I'd like to hire you. Are you available at the present time, or do you have a client," she asked?

"I have a client, but if what you need me for doesn't involve too much, I could manage it. What did you have in mind," I asked?

"Someone broke into my doctor's office and stole my medical records about three days ago. The police are looking into it, but they've already informed me that they doubt very seriously they'll find the records or the one who stole them. Could you look into it for me," Ann-Margret asked?

This came as a bolt of lightning out of the blue. Someone stole Ann-Margret's medical records. I started to answer when I noticed the look on Juliet's face. She was staring at Ann-Margret in stunned disbelief.

"Someone stole your medical records," Juliet said questioningly?

"Yes...oh, I guess I didn't tell you, did I," Ann-Margret replied.

"This is bizarre. Someone stole mine as well. Do you go to Dr. Wellman over on Sunset Blvd," Juliet asked?

"Yes...don't tell me he's your doctor, too," Ann-Margret said displaying her surprise?

"He has been for over three years. What is going on? Mine were stolen at the same time as yours, it seems," Juliet stated.

"Well, if I find one I'll find the other one's records, as well," I stated and then added. "You can split the cost; how's that?"

The two women looked at one another for a moment and then broke into light laughter. I wasn't sure what they had seen that was so funny, but I went along with the laughter as though I did.

It was at this point that I heard another familiar voice from behind me; one I recognized instantly. Before I had a chance to turn around the man moved up to the table where I could see him.

"Well, hello ladies...gentleman," John Wayne said.

I looked up at him, but he wasn't interested in me. "Hello, Duke," Juliet and Ann-Margret replied at the same time with big smiles.

"Maureen and I were just wondering what you two are working on; care to share; or is it a secret," the Duke asked with a smile of his own?

"I have several movies in the works, Duke," Ann-Margret said. "One is called the 'Pleasure Seekers'; the others really haven't been titled yet."

"What about you, Juliet," Wayne asked?

"Right now I'm working on my Vegas act. I hope you'll be able to catch it. What about you," Juliet asked?

"I just finished 'The Sons of Katie Elder' with Dean Martin and then went right to work on 'In Harms Way'. I'll tell you the truth; I'm bushed," he grinned.

"I think we all know that feeling," he women laughed.

"Well, I just wanted to say hi. We'll all have to do a movie together someday," he said sincerely.

"That would be a lot of fun," both women agreed.

It was only then that he looked down at me and said, "I don't think we met; if we did I didn't caught your name," Wayne said, wrinkling his forehead and flashing a half smile.

"Weigel, Sean Weigel, Mr. Wayne," I replied.

He held out a massive hand to shake and I took it expecting a crushing handshake. He held off much to my delight. I swear he could have crushed every bone in my hand.

"Are you in show biz," he asked?

"No, I'm a private investigator," I replied.

"A gumshoe, huh. Great job; one I might have done if I hadn't gotten into movies. It's nice to have met you, Weigel. Well, I'd better report back to Maureen; goodbye all," he said with a smile and walked back to the table he was sharing with Maureen O'Hara.

"I should have asked him if his medical records had been stolen," I said thoughtfully.

"I pity anyone who would steal 'anything' from the Duke. He'd hunt them down and then mop up the city with them," Juliet said with a laugh and being joined by Ann-Margret.

121

17

BEFORE the two ladies left they both gave me phone numbers where they could be reached. I'd picked up two new clients and figured that when I found one's medical records I'd find the other's as well.

After my two gorgeous new clients had left, I sat there for sometime contemplating the connection; if there was one; between Elvis's dental records being stolen and Ann-Margret and Juliet Prowse's medical records being filched. I doubted seriously that it was just a coincidence.

Both women had made movies with Elvis, so I figured it had to have something to do with that fact. As I sat there contemplating what I'd learned one thought kept creeping to the front of my thought processing line.

It was common knowledge around Hollywood that Elvis was quite the ladies man. He was notorious for having affairs with the women who co-starred with him in his movies. Of course, he was not the only one who could make that claim.

One way to find out if the other medical thefts had something to do with Elvis, would be to check on the other women appearing in movies with him, and see if any of them had their medical records pilfered recently as well. If so, then the thefts could only be for one purpose...blackmail. The medical files would show any uncelebrated and unplanned pregnancies the women stars might have had and kept from the public.

With Hollywood being the hub of movie making around the world, and the stars being set on ivory towers, a scandal; any scandal; was big news. Where there is big news, there's usually big money to be made.

This whole crazy thing about replacing Elvis with his twin brother had gotten out of control. There were two murders the police were working on and they both could lead them to this Elvis counterfeiting scheme of the Colonel's. I had to make sure my hands were clean or I'd go down the gutter with everyone else.

Suddenly I remembered something. One of Elvis's co-stars had entered a convent not too long after she had co-starred in, not one, but two Elvis movies. At first I couldn't remember her name, but knew that she had become a nun. It had come as a shock to the movie insiders because she had such a promising movie career when she donned the nun's habit.

I sat there for several long, thoughtful moments until the name Dolores Hart popped into my head. I wondered if anyone had tried to snatch her medical records. The only way I would find that out would be to find out who her doctor was while she was here in Hollywood and go check with him.

A simple phone call would remedy that little problem. I asked the waiter for a phone and when he brought one to my table, I dialed my Hollywood 'dirt' source, Pete Stallone. If there was dirt on anyone in Hollywood, Pete would know it; if it was knowable, that is. Hopefully he wouldn't know anything about an Elvis switch.

The phone rang five times before Pete picked up on the other end. He sounded sleepy, which was only natural since he did most of his business after dark.

"Say, Pete...did I wake you? This is Sean," I said unable to hold back a grin.

"No, that's all right, Sean. I had to get up to answer the phone anyway," he joked. "What's up?"

"I've been hired to locate some missing medical reports and wondered if you'd picked up any scuttlebutt on heists of that nature," I asked, unsure of what I might learn from the 'ears of Hollywood rumblings'.

He paused for a moment before saying, "Drop the case, Sean!"

"What...why, what have you heard," I asked, a serious frown distorting my face.

"This has to do with several of the major studios wanting to stop the exodus of their money making stars who want to go independent," Pete said, actually lowering his voice as he spoke.

"You mean they want to threaten them with going public with any health issues they might have to keep them in the fold? I don't see where that would be a big hammer hanging over their heads," I replied.

"It is if the hammer has a diaper wrapped around it. At least that's the way it is for the women; the men it's a paternity suit," Pete said and then paused before giving me some more juicy information.

"Sean...did you know that five of the studios have gone together and set up an adoption agency named 'Children of the World Adoption Center'?"

"No, how long has this been around," I asked ponderously?

"I only learned about it a year ago and I know better than to make it public knowledge. In fact, you're the only person I've shared this bit of info with and that's only because I know I can trust you to keep it quiet. These big boys play rough...and they play for keeps, if you get my drift," Pete said with the whispered voice again.

"Pete, this is huge. So what you're saying is if one of their stars was to get knocked up she could have the baby and it would be adopted out; all under the cover of darkness, so to speak," I said.

"You've got it. The adoption center has a team of doctors who can perform abortions if the actress doesn't want to actually give birth to the baby," Pete went on.

"So if a woman wants to go independent they steal her medical records to stop her from leaving. I can see that if the woman has a history of medical problems she doesn't want the public to know about, but not so much the adoption aspect of it," I said thoughtfully.

"Have you ever heard of forgery? They merely 'doctor up' the medical files with things they want to appear in them and then force the woman to stay with them," Pete said evenly.

"I can certainly understand the women who have played the adoption game not wanting that to come out," I answered, thinking about the Presley situation.

"Did you know there was a dentist killed last night," Pete said, "a Doctor Early?"

I started to say yes, but caught myself in time, "No, is that significant in some way?"

"It may be. The doctor had a number of high profile movie and television stars. He's John Wayne's dentist, as well as Paul Newman's and Elvis Presley's. I can't say for sure it's connected, but I hear from my sources down at police headquarters that a number of files were taken," Pete said.

"Hmm, that is interesting," I said knowingly and then asked him, "Pete, what can you tell me about the actress Dolores Hart...anything?"

"What is it you want to know, Sean? Why did she give up movies for a convent?"

"Yeah, something like that. I hear she was engaged at the time she made her decision."

"Yeah, she was; and she had also had a very heated affair with one Elvis Presley. They tried to keep it covered up, but from what I hear she was mighty upset when he dropped her for another beauty."

"Is that right; I hadn't heard that," I said thoughtfully.

"Anything else I can help you out with Sean," Pete asked?

"No, not that I can think of right now," I said and then added, "Hey, Pete thanks a lot. I'll drop a little something to you in the mail."

"It will be appreciated, Sean; you know that," Pete said.

"Go back to bed and I'll talk to you later," I said and we hung up.

Pete had given me a lot more information than I had counted on. This whole case was turning into a Pandora's Box of worms. I had always known Hollywood held secrets that could make or break people and their careers in a heart beat, but it was even worse than I'd originally thought.

I remembered how RKO Studios had been rumored to have gotten Robert Mitchum busted on a marijuana charge, merely to teach him a lesson for his rebellious conduct. There had been rumors about possible murders having been committed to bring an end to an overly hard to handle star, but without any hard evidence to back up the rumored claims.

One thing you don't want to do when you're working around high profile celebrities, be it movie stars or politicians, is step on too many toes. And believe me, there are some mighty big toes that could and should be stepped on. I'd heard and seen things that I knew to be true, but valued my career and my life to a point of keeping my ears open and my mouth shut.

Knowing how the studios worked, I knew that if they wanted someone silenced they had the clout to make it happen...permanently. I also knew of some politicians that could and would do the same thing, only quicker. I also had my suspicions about Colonel Tom Parker.

18

PETE STALLONE had given me a 'full' plate of information' to ponder. Why had Dolores Hart quit the movies and joined the nunnery? It bothered me; not so much that she took religion over a movie career, but the manner in which she did it.

Dolores had only made nine movies when she bolted from Hollywood. She was being groomed for stardom and they were bringing her along at an even pace. Miss Hart had co-starred with some of Hollywood's bigger names, plus she had held her own in the acting department; so why the sudden switch?

A trip to a small shop on Sunset Blvd answered a few more questions for me. The shop owner collected trivia on everything from movies to television to radio. The trivia covered everything from acting to sports to politics. The storeowner, Benny Hutchens was an old friend of mine and when it came to 'known' trivia, had a leg up on Pete Stallone.

Benny had just finished with a good looking female customer who gave me an appraising eye when I walked up to where she and Benny were standing.

"Well, hello Sean. How's tricks," Benny said with his ever ready smile?

"Fine, Benny, but I didn't mean to interrupt you. Go ahead with the lady," I said thoughtfully.

"Oh, we're through," the woman said lowering her eyelids and giving that smoldering look.

"That's too bad; I was going to just stand here and enjoy the view," I said, turning on the 'old charm'.

She liked the compliment and grinned seductively as she picked up the paper bag of goodies she'd bought and started for the door.

Saying it loud enough for her to hear my comment, but not too loud, I said, "The view is great both coming and going."

A quick glance back confirmed to me that she'd heard my comment. Benny stood there shaking his head slowly from side to side.

"I wish I had your gift of gab, or is it line of BS," he asked jokingly?

"Even I haven't figured that out yet, Benny," I replied.

"So what brings you in to see old Benny Boy," he asked?

"I'm looking for some trivia on Dolores Hart. What can you dig up for me?"

"What do you want to know," he asked?

I looked questioningly at him and asked curiously, "You mean you know trivia about her right off the top of your little 'pea picking head',"

"Hey, I should be able to remember something about her, seeing as how I had a request for info on her just two days ago," Benny replied and then had his own question. "What makes her such a hot trivia topic all of a sudden," he asked?

"That's what I'd like to know," I replied.

"Here's what I've got," he started and gave me mostly what I already knew.

Then he gave me something I didn't know.

"She was engaged to a guy by the name of Don Robinson when she suddenly, and quite unexpectedly left Hollywood and joined the Abbey of Regina Laudis. They're still friends from what insiders have told me," Benny stated.

"Don Robinson, eh," I said, making a mental note of the man's name.

"What else do you want to know about Sister Hart," Benny asked?

"Actually that last bit of information helps me greatly, Benny; thank you, partner," I said.

Benny looked past me and said quietly, "It looks like you've found an admirer, Sean."

I gave a quick glance over my shoulder and the good looking lady who Benny had been waiting on when I entered was lingering at a rack of old magazines near the door. It was obvious she wasn't interested in buying any of the reading material; she kept casting little glances our way.

"Well, it looks like things might get interesting, Benny. If you don't hear from me in a couple of weeks, call the police and tell them to send out a search party with more ice," I said jokingly.

133

Benny caught my meaning and chuckled. We said goodbye and I headed out the door. As I neared the magazine rack the woman moved backwards causing me to bump into her.

"Oh, I'm sorry," I said sincerely. "Are you all right," I asked?

"I've been told I'm better than 'all right'; I've been told I'm sensational," she said giving me that look that has pillows and sheets written all over it.

"I'll just bet you are," I said and gave her my 'Oil Can Harry' grin.

You know who 'Oil Can Harry' was, don't you? He was the feline villain in the Mighty Mouse cartoons. Anyway, she knew who he was because her next line proved it.

"If I told you I was very vulnerable when it comes to big, strong, virile men...you wouldn't take it the wrong way would you?"

"That all depends on what the wrong way is," I grinned coyly.

"I mean, you wouldn't try to seduce me...would you," she purred?

"No...I wouldn't try...I would," I said dropping my smile and giving her my Cary Grant stare.

"I was hoping you'd say that," she smiled; took me by the tie, and led me out the door to her 1964 red Corvette that was parked in front of my car.

"Where are you parked," she asked?

"Right behind you, Baby," I said and motioned towards my 1960 Chevy Impala.

"Oh, you know my name...good. Follow me," she said as she let go of my tie and walked around to the driver's side of the Corvette.

I hurried around and climbed into my car and followed her as she pulled into traffic. We drove about eight blocks and she turned into an underground parking garage at the Haven View Apartments.

I found a parking spot at the curb right in front of the main entrance to the apartment building and started walking towards the garage entrance. I heard the sound of a car slowing down and turned and looked back towards the street.

Quite by accident I saw the gun barrel sticking out the passenger's side window of the black Lincoln which probably saved my life. Out of shear instinct I dived to the ground as a volley of gunshots rang out. The bullets pinged off the concrete walkway on both sides of me.

I pulled my .38 Smith and Wesson and fired three shots at the Lincoln as it quickly accelerated and sped away. As I got to my feet, my new blonde friend came running up to where I was, her eyes as big as saucers.

"Oh, my Gosh...are you all right," she asked excitedly?

"Yeah, other than being a little shook up," I answered. "I hope that wasn't a jealous boyfriend...or worse yet, husband," I said.

"No, I'm unattached at the present. None of my men friends would do anything like that, I can assure you," Baby said and paused. "What line of work are you in, anyway?"

"I'm a private cop," I said.

"I was referring to your occupation; oh, so were you," she said with a wry smile.

135

This woman was smoldering hot. She needed to take a cold shower; and so did I.

"Maybe I should have said that I'm a private investigator," I replied.

"And if I was to hire your services and looked in the yellow pages under private investigators, what name would I look for," she asked?

"That all depends on what you wanted investigated," I replied checking the street to make sure my friends in the black Lincoln were not making a return trip.

"Let's say I wanted you to investigate...oh, I don't know...me; what name would I be looking for?"

"Sean Weigel. And if I answered my phone and it was you calling, what name would you give me," I asked, playing her little word game?

She paused for several moments before saying quietly, "Baby," and took me by the tie again and led me towards the front entrance of the apartment building.

I was so glad I wasn't wearing a clip on tie at the time, but rather, one that actually went around my neck.

19

THE SHOOTING INCIDENT told me someone wasn't too happy with my snooping around. Now the question was simple, who, what, and why. Who was it I was asking questions about that would warrant the other 'who' to put a hit out on me. The 'what' was the 'what' reason the questions were causing such a violent reaction? And, the 'why' would be answered when I discovered the 'who' and 'what'.

I've always loved a good mystery and I had worked myself into the middle of a great one. I might have incurred the wrath of some studio bosses, or perhaps some secret agency that didn't like my snooping around because I might uncover something on them. The thought even crossed my mind that it might be Colonel Tom Parker wanting to make sure I never talked, now that I'd found Jesse Garon for him.

The one person I felt was not responsible for any of the killings or the attempted silencing of me was Elvis himself. I knew enough about the man to consider him a safe bet as not being involved in any of the incidents. The Colonel was a different story, however.

I knew that I'd have to keep on my toes if I was to stay alive now. These guys, whoever they were, were playing for keeps. Another thing I knew for sure was that I'd need all the firepower I could muster. I'd have to make sure I put my .45 automatic in the secret compartment under my car's glove box.

I finally left Baby's place at around eleven o'clock that night and headed for home, but with one stop along the way. I wanted to see a friend of mine who was loosely tied to several covert operation groups; a guy by the name of Leonel Martinez.

Martinez was involved in the failed Bay of Pigs Operation. He had barely escaped with his life and eventually made his way back to the United States. Once here he had connected to the CIA sponsored DRF; the Democratic Revolutionary Front.

When funding for the DRF and the CRC, the 'Cuban Revolutionary Council' was cut, he and Jose' Miro' Cordona's right hand man, Carlos Pintero, moved to Los Angeles and went underground. Cordona had been the chairman of the CRC. It was a good bet he was still on the payroll of the CIA.

Martinez had become well known in certain circles as a man to be feared. He would hire out as a hit man as long as the targets were known KGB agents or Cuban loyalists to the Castro regime. Of course there was no hard evidence that could be used against him. Leonel and the CIA saw to that.

I'd met him quite by accident when I stopped on the shoulder of the Santa Ana Freeway and helped him deliver a baby; his and his wife's first child. He said he would be eternally grateful and I believed he would be.

I pulled up across the street from the club called 'The Havana Club' and parked. The club was a rough looking place that usually had at least one visit a night by the cops. I hoped they'd already had their quota of trouble for the night.

There were three Cuban men standing outside the club as I made my way across the street to the club's entrance. They all three gave me hard stares as I neared the door. I knew they didn't like Gringos coming into their clubs, but I was there on business.

"Where are you going," one of the men asked me?

I ignored him and put my hand on the door to push it open. He spoke again, only louder this time.

"Hey, Gringo...where do you think you are going?"

I looked at him with a deep frown as I said, "I came to see Leonel Martinez if you must know."

The man's eyes widened as he stiffened slightly. He looked quickly at the other two and then back at me.

"Oh, I was just wondering, that is all," he said apologetically.

"I thought that was it," I said.

I went on inside and stopped to give the bar the once over. I spotted Leonel sitting with two other men at the back of the club. Making my way along the bar I could feel the penetrating looks I was receiving from the bar's patrons as I walked towards the back.

Leonel had his head down as he talked with the two men. When I was about eight feet from the table Leonel looked up with a scowl on his face; but when he saw it was me, the scowl became a wide smile.

"Well, well, if it isn't my old friend Dr. Sean Weigel; how are you doing good doctor," Leonel asked opening his arms wide?

"I'm fine Leonel, just fine. I was merely checking to see if you had any more babies to be delivered," I joked.

"No, not at the present, but I will see what I can do in about nine months from now," he said going along with the joke.

Leonel's smile slowly faded and he turned a little more serious as he asked, "So what is it brings you to 'The Havana Club' my friend?"

"I was just wondering if you might know who would want to take a shot at a lowly private investigator like myself," I said dropping my own smile.

Leonel frowned slightly, "Oh, someone does not like you stepping on their toes with your questions?"

"It looks that way. The case I was hired for has no reason for someone to use me as target practice," I said evenly, and then added, "I'd like to know who tried to kill me tonight."

"I have heard nothing through the grapevine from any of my contacts. You are not working on something involving a politician, are you?

"No, Hollywood types, but no politicians," I replied.

"That can be almost as bad," Leonel said and then added. "Many of the studio heads are loyal to Castro. They are also very friendly with Soviet operatives. I know this for a fact," Leonel said with a knowing look.

"I guess what you're saying is that I'd better watch my step when dealing with the studios. I'll do that. Oh, by the way...how is your lovely wife? And, the little ones of course," I asked?

Leonel smiled, "They are fine. The children number three now; and Sean is a good boy. I'll tell them you asked about them," Leonel said and then looked at the other men at the table, signaling to me that they were in a serious discussion and I should leave.

"Adios, my friend," I said and walked out of the club.

It was clear that my questions were not being well received around Hollywood. Perhaps I'd better concentrate more on doing Elvis's business, but how could I turn my back on the likes of Ann-Margret and Juliet Prowse...I couldn't and wouldn't.

I went on home and straight to bed. I had several people I wanted to talk with the next day; actually that day, by the time I hit the hay; it was 1:00 am. One of the people was a friend of mine on the LA Police force; Bruce Lansford.

20

LT. BRUCE LANSFORD looked up from a stack of paperwork on his desk and smiled when he recognized me.

"Well, hello Sean. What brings you down here to where real police work is done," Bruce grinned.

"Donuts...I need a donut," I laughed.

"That old joke needs to be revised. I've heard that from everyone I meet...including my wife," Bruce said joining me in laughter.

"Actually I was wondering what you have on the Dr. Early murder I read about in the newspaper. I have a client who was good friends with the doctor and was just curious," I lied.

Bruce looked around to see if anyone was listening and said under his breath, "We think the killer may have actually been questioned by the first ones on the scene, but slipped away. He gave them a statement, but the custodial service said they don't have anyone by the name he gave officers, on their payroll. His address didn't check out either."

"Hmm; and the ones who questioned him don't have any idea who he is," I asked curiously?

"Not a clue. They couldn't even agree on how tall the guy was. I know what you're going to say, but don't. These things happen once in awhile," Bruce said with a frown.

"Maybe the one they questioned wasn't involved in the doctor's murder, either; did you think of that?"

"Yeah, that could be. But, if not, then why was he busy cleaning offices on the top floor of the building," Bruce replied?

"Maybe he had a cleaning fetish," I grinned.

"Ha, ha," Bruce said mockingly.

"I don't know if you got a call on this or not, but I'll run it by you, anyway. Did you get any calls about a shooting incident yesterday? It would have been outside the Haven View Apartments," I offered?

"A shooting...was anyone hurt," Bruce asked?

"No, not that I know of," I replied.

Bruce shook his head negatively, "No, I don't recall an incident call coming in for that area. Wait a minute and I'll check," he said.

"You don't have to," I started to say, but it was too late to stop Bruce.

"Hey, Chet...did we get any calls about a shooting incident at Haven View Apartments yesterday," he called to another officer?

"No, I can tell you that for sure. I just went over all incoming calls on shootings yesterday and there was nothing for that area," the officer named Chet said.

Bruce looked at me, "Did you get that, Sean?"

"Yep, I was just wondering," I said, not wanting to go into details.

Just then a call came in on Bruce's phone. He picked up and began speaking to the person on the other end. The look he gave me told me he was going to be awhile, so I gave him a wave and headed for the door. Passing by a small table near the door I did pick a donut out of the large cardboard container of various pastries that was on it.

It didn't bother me that no one had reported the shooting incident at the apartment complex. Of course, had I been wounded it would have been nice to know that someone cared enough to phone the police.

One thing was for sure; I was a lot more alert about things going on around me now. I didn't want to make myself an easy target by walking around with my head in a cloud.

I went to my office and found a message from Colonel Parker. He wanted me to meet him at a house located on Topanga Canyon Road by twelve noon. I knew the area well enough to know about where the house was located. I wondered if that was his house or just one he'd rented to house Jesse Garon aka Danny Breedlove in. It turned out to be the latter.

There were only two vehicles at the house in Topanga Canyon when I arrived there. I figured one was the Colonel's and the other belonged to Elvis. My car looked a little out of place next to those two, I thought.

I rang the bell and Vernon Presley opened the door as though he'd been waiting for me. He greeted me warmly and ushered me into a large den equipped with games, television, a pool table and a shuffle board; not to mention a full sized bar.

Elvis and Danny were no where to be seen, but I figured they were in the house. When Elvis entered the room, followed closely by Jesse, my mouth dropped open wide enough to place a small hamburger in.

Elvis, I think it was, greeted me with a smile and a handshake. The Colonel was busy talking on the phone but did give me a wave. I was so stunned I plopped down on a huge sofa that was so comfortable I'd be happy with my carcass parked on it for the rest of the day.

I literally could not tell the two men apart. Jesse's hair had been dyed to match Elvis's and he was wearing Elvis's signature cool looking clothes. They both looked great and exactly alike.

"So what do you think, Mr. Weigel," the one I figured to be Elvis asked?

"You look like a mirror image of each other, Elvis," I said.

The man I had addressed grinned, "I'm Danny...uh, Jesse."

I looked at the other man and nodded towards him, "Elvis?"

Elvis grinned as he nodded his answer.

"Man, oh man. This is phenomenal," was all I could say.

"What do you want to drink, Mr. Weigel," Elvis asked? "We've got just about anything you might like."

"How about a cup of coffee," I replied.

"Oh, we don't have any of that," Elvis said seriously and held the look for a few seconds before he and Jesse broke into laughter.

"One cup of coffee coming up; how do you want it," Elvis then asked?

"Hot and black," I said.

Elvis got me a cup of coffee and set it on the coffee table in front of me. He also moved a box of pastries from the bar over to the coffee table.

"I hope you'll excuse us, Mr. Weigel, but Jesse and I are working on some songs," Elvis smiled.

"Oh, go ahead. But, please...call me Sean," I answered.

"Okay, call me Elvis...for the time being," he grinned and then added. "I want you to listen to this song."

Elvis walked over to a large tape recorder and switched it on. He and Jesse picked up microphones and listened for their cue. The song was 'Don't Be Cruel'.

Elvis called to me while the intro music was playing, "Turn around and don't look and tell me what you think when it's over."

I turned around and one of them started singing. I listened intently to the entire song. When it ended I turned around and looked at two smiling faces. Elvis then gave an infectious chuckle, and asked me a question I could not honestly answer.

"Who started the song? Was it me or Jesse," he asked?

I grinned as I took a guess, "You," I said.

"Huh uh...it was Jesse. Who sang the second verse," Elvis asked?

"Jesse," I guessed again.

"Nope, it was me. Who sang the entire ending of the song; Jesse or me," he asked?

"You," I said thinking I had guessed right.

"We both did, alternating lines," Elvis laughed.

I honestly could not tell the difference in the two voices. I could have watched them and not been able to tell them apart; visually or audibly.

For the first time I felt that the exchange of the original 'Elvis' for the counterfeit Elvis would work. Jesse said that the things Elvis did subconsciously were much like his own idiosyncrasies; ones he had been forced to subdue to keep from being accused of trying to act like Elvis while growing up in Houston.

"We've got just about all the songs down all ready because Jesse knows most of them," Elvis said almost giddy as he explained things.

I could see that both of them were ecstatic about having been united through this 'venture'. I had the feeling that it wouldn't matter to either of them if this thing blew up in their faces just as long as they were together, literally for the first time.

About this time the Colonel finished his phone conversation and joined us. He had a scowl on his face as he looked from Elvis and Jesse to Vernon and then finally to me.

"We've got trouble," he said finally, "Someone has found out about our little plan."

"Oh," I said, "Is that what the phone call was all about?"

"Yes. That guy that was murdered at the studio the other day left a tape recording in his apartment exposing what we were planning on doing with Jesse. I was lucky that one of my men was able to get to it before the police found it," the Colonel stated.

"How'd you find out about the murder in time to get someone over to his place before the police got there," I wondered aloud?

"I have eyes and ears all over Hollywood, my boy," the Colonel said, and then dropped a bombshell.

"I even know that someone has been following you and tried to kill you yesterday. I don't know who they are yet, and was hoping you might be able to tell me who they are; can you?"

"No, I can't," I said with a frown and then snapped. "Isn't it a little odd that you know about the shooting, but the police don't?"

"Not at all, my boy; there are crimes committed everyday; hell, every hour, every minute, that the guilty parties know all about, but the police don't have a clue until someone tells them about it," the Colonel replied.

"Do you have someone tailing me," I asked seriously?

"No, I do not...well, sort of. I wanted to see what you would do once we'd made our agreement for permanent employment. I was pleased to see

149

that you were having lunch with some of Elvis's lady friends. I take it you didn't say anything about our little secret," he grinned?

"You know I didn't, or you would have ripped into me as soon as I walked in here," I countered his question.

"You're right there. I hear that several people have had medical records stolen from their doctor's office; what do you know about that," the Colonel asked?

"Man, you do have eyes and ears everywhere, don't you," I said before answering his question. "I know that Ann-Margret and Juliet Prowse both had their medical records stolen. I'm wondering about Dolores Hart's records also. I'll bet you twenty bucks that her medical records have been lifted as well," I said.

"All three of them were in movies with Elvis. I wonder if someone is...," the Colonel said thoughtfully, but stopped short of finishing his self directed query?

"Trying to find a connection between the woman and an unannounced pregnancy," I said, finishing his sentence for him. "That was my first thought," I stated.

"I can tell you there were no pregnancies," the Colonel snapped.

"I have heard that the studios have set up an adoption agency under a fictitious name so they can handle any unwanted pregnancies. The agency also handles abortions. Have you heard anything about that," I asked?

"I wouldn't go that route Mr. Weigel. It could lead to a very 'dead' end," the Colonel said without benefit of smile and emphasizing the word 'dead'.

"Maybe it's someone from the studios who tried to bring my investigation to an abrupt end," I said, making sure he understood me. "Let me tell you something, Colonel; I don't like being threatened. And I sure don't like being shot at. Not 'if' I find the guilty party, but when I find them someone is going to pay through the nose for what they've done."

"I hear that you are taking the two ladies on as clients. Is that right," Colonel Tom asked?

How did he know that, I wondered to myself as I answered, "Yes, I am! To be honest, I figure that if I find their files I'll also find Elvis's dental records," I said evenly.

"I hope so. Keep me posted on all counts," the Colonel ordered.

He turned around and walked back to where the phone was, picked it up and dialed some telephone number. Elvis and Jesse were going over photographs and Elvis was explaining all he could about the people in the pictures.

I left with a simple wave towards Elvis, Jesse, and the Colonel. Vernon Presley saw me to the door. When we reached the door he looked back at his two sons and said, "I think those two boys in there are in hog heaven. I tell you, Sean, I truly wish their mama could be here to witness this," Vernon said.

151

"I'm sure you do. But, maybe she had a little something to do in setting it up; we don't know," I grinned.

"It would be just like her," he grinned.

"How did Jesse take the news about being adopted by the Breedlove couple? Did he seem upset by it all," I asked?

"He was stunned; but he said they had been like his real mama and daddy and he was grateful because of the love they showered him with. He's got a good head on his shoulder. You can certainly tell the two of them are twins; and I don't mean the way they look and sing. I'm talking about the way they think, as well."

All I could do with that bit of news was smile. Reunions are great; especially when it involves one's who thought the other was dead. I'd have to think that might be the way it is in heaven; one great big, happy reunion. I hope so, anyway.

21

I HEADED down the canyon keeping an eye out for any suspicious looking cars that might start tailing me. I didn't notice any until I reached Topanga Canyon Blvd. That was when I noticed a dark colored sedan pull from the shoulder of the road and start following me, staying a ways back so as not to be too obvious.

I kept a watchful eye on the car hoping to find the right moment to lose them. It came when I met three truck and trailers headed in the opposite direction. Waiting until the last possible second, I suddenly crimped the steering wheel hard to the left and did a 180 degree spin around, cutting in front of the lead truck.

By the time the car following me could react the other two big rigs were too close for the car to turn around. They had to wait until the trucks passed them by and then made their U turn. By that time I had headed up the road with the 'pedal to the metal'. I spotted just the place to turn out and pulled in behind a parked delivery van.

The car that had been following me sped by within a minute or so and as soon as it did, I headed back the other way towards my office. I love it when I lose a tail like that. I knew they'd find me again though. I'm in the phone book.

When I got back to my office I had a message from Pete Stallone. He left a phone number with Jodi, my secretary and told her he had some information for me. I quickly dialed the number he'd left.

"Harvey's Bar and Grill," a man's voice said.

"Hi, my name is Sean Weigel; is Pete Stallone there," I asked?

"Pete...yeah, he was here just a minute ago; I saw him talking to two guys near the juke box," the man I presumed to be the bartender said.

"Hey, does anybody know where Pete Stallone is," the bartender yelled?

After a couple of seconds he said, "Someone said Pete left with the two guys I saw him talking to. Do you want to leave a message?"

"If he comes back in just tell him that Sean called. He'll know who you're talking about. Tell him I'll give him a call later tonight," I said.

"Sure thing...oh, is this Sean Weigel," the bartender asked?

"Yes, that's me," I answered.

"Pete said that if he missed you for me to tell you to be on your toes and check out a guy named Grant Corning. Pete thinks he might have the answers you're looking for," the bartender stated.

"Grant Corning...thanks; thanks a lot," I said.

The name Grant Corning rang a bell, but I couldn't remember where I'd heard it; when I'd heard it; or in relation to what. For some reason it seemed like it had to do with an extortion ring the cops had broken up several years back, but I couldn't be sure. A trip to the LA Times would take care of that, though.

I left a note for my AWOL secretary and headed to the newspaper office. I went to the archive department and filled out a form explaining what it was I was looking for and wrote down Grant Corning as the subject in question.

The woman went to a large filing cabinet and began to look for anything they had on Corning. Within a couple of minutes she came back and brought me a newspaper that had a story in it referring to Grant Corning.

I'd been right; he had been involved in an extortion ring, but had gotten off Scot free when the key witness was killed by a hit and run driver. Grant Corning was the man the gang used for strong arming their victims.

After reading about the guy, I suddenly had a bad feeling about Pete Stallone. The bartender had said he left with two guys unknown to him. I hoped one of the guys wasn't Mr. Grant Corning.

I noticed that the arresting officer in the case was none other than one of my old nemesis by the name of Allen Baldwin. We'd locked horns on numerous occasions simply because he didn't like private cops. He had tried to have my license lifted several times but had been unsuccessful, which only made him hate me all the more.

A smile worked its way across my face as I thought of the look on Baldwin's face when I showed up at police headquarters and started asking him questions about Corning's arrest. He would howl like a banshee.

Hopefully Baldwin would tell me what he knew about Corning's current activities. It was my guess that the strong arm specialist was still involved in the same thing he'd done back when he got busted. It was undoubtedly a profession he excelled in.

Baldwin was talking to two other detectives when I entered the squad room. He didn't see me until I was standing next to him. When he glanced my way, he did a double take and then spat, "What do you want here, Weigel?"

"You, old chap, you," I said, getting a grin from the other two detectives.

"It'll be a cold day in hell when I give you any help on a case; it that's what you're doing here," he said almost spitting the words at me.

"Now come on Al, let's shake hands and start all over," I offered, knowing he wouldn't go along with my proposal.

"If we shake hands...I'll come out fighting. Look Weigel...I don't like you and I wouldn't help you solve a case if it was on the President of the USA. Now get out of here," Baldwin snapped.

"Okay, I'll see you around. I'll go to the Times and tell them that I wanted to give this information to the police, but Lt. Allen Baldwin wasn't interested in it," I threatened.

"Okay, okay...what is it you want? And it had better not be something that requires that I spend very much time on it," Baldwin said.

"I see. You wouldn't want another crack at Grant Corning, huh," I asked nonchalantly?

"Corning? What have you got to do with that dirt bag," Baldwin snapped?

"I think he's getting back into the strong arm business," I said proudly.

Baldwin's eyes lit up momentarily. He hated Grant Corning and didn't hesitate to let his hatred be known. And, he didn't care who was within earshot when expressing his hatred for the man.

I had always thought Baldwin could wind up a prime target for a frame up. All a person would have to do would be to make sure Baldwin had no alibi for the time they bumped off Corning and the cop would be the prime suspect. The prosecutor could march a cast of thousands through the court room who would swear they'd heard Baldwin threaten Corning over the years.

Baldwin looked at me with a serious eye before saying, "What is it you want to know about him?"

"Where he lives, for one thing; also, the names of some of those he was involved with in the extortion ring. I'm working on a case that might have something for you to sink your teeth into and would be your main course. You can save me a lot of time and that will get you involved that much quicker," I stated.

That was all I had to say for him to spring into action. Within five minutes I had a ton of information on Corning. This marked the first time that Baldwin had ever given me anything helpful on a case I was involved in. This proved that Baldwin hated Corning a little more than me.

I left police headquarters with a file folder full of information on Corning, but I'd had to promise in front of witnesses that I'd provide Baldwin with any information I turned up on the guy. I wouldn't mind keeping that promise because that would put the burden of busting Corning and anyone he might be involved with on the police; mainly Baldwin. I'd have to make sure that Baldwin didn't know anything about the 'counterfeit Elvis' scheme, though.

I swung back by my office and dropped off the file and found a message to contact the Colonel again. He wanted to let me know that the work with Danny had gotten underway, and he'd be in and out of town for awhile. He said he'd give me a call as soon as he got back in the LA area.

I called it an evening and went home. When I got there I gave my new friend, Baby, a call. There was no answer. I opened a beer and turned on the television to watch the news. When I woke up my beer was warm and a test pattern was on the tube.

I looked at my watch and it was 3:45 am. I got up off the sofa and went to bed. I didn't realize I was so tired, because I went right back to sleep and didn't wake up until around 6:30 am.

Los Angeles, CA
July, 26, 1965

It had been two weeks since returning to LA with Danny Breedlove and I was still no closer to finding out who stole Elvis's dental file, or the medical records of Ann-Margret and Juliet Prowse. I kept hitting one dead end after another. It was as if I was in a hockey game and someone kept changing the rules of the game without telling me which kept me in the penalty box.

I met with both Ann-Margret and Juliet several times, but pulled myself off their payrolls due to no conclusive findings on my part. I told them any investigating I did on the medical records would be my contribution to the movie industry. I continued to follow leads, but with no positive findings.

On July 26th I got a message from the Colonel telling me he wanted me to come to the house on Topanga Canyon Road the next morning. He said to be there by 8 am and not to be late.

I asked him if he had ever gotten a ransom note for the files, or any kind of contact that might indicate a blackmail scheme. He said he'd received nothing; nothing, that is but a few offers for Elvis appearances on various television shows that were in trouble and wanted Elvis for a walk-on to boost their sagging ratings.

I always got a queasy feeling in the pit of my stomach, when having to meet with the Colonel. Perhaps it was due to all the things I'd heard about the man; most of which were somewhat true. But some things were a little over the top.

When I went to bed the night before the meeting, I made sure my alarm clock was set as well as leaving a 'wake up call' with my answering service.

It was a good thing my answering service was on the ball because the alarm clock didn't go off. I hate the clocks that have both an am and a pm setting. I had set it for 6 pm instead of 6 am. Hey, I'm a good investigator, not an engineer.

22

July 27, 1965
Topanga Canyon Rd.

THE DRIVEWAY at the house on Topanga Canyon Road was jammed with vehicles when I arrived there. I managed to find a spot on the shoulder of the road in front of the house and made my way through the cars to the front door.

Again, Vernon Presley opened the door and greeted me. The house was noisy with all the chatter from Elvis's entourage, both men and women; you could tell they all got along with one another. These were all the people most closely connected to Elvis. Vernon took me around and introduced me to all the guys.

"So, what line of work are you in, Sean," Red West asked me.

"I'm a private investigator," I replied wondering how that would go over with the Memphis crowd.

"Really; man, I'll bet that's an interesting job, huh? Have you worked on any high profile cases," he asked, truly interested?

"No, all of mine are low profile. My clients usually don't want any publicity attached to their cases and that's what they get when they hire me; low profile," I said truthfully.

Red looked at me quizzically and then towards the Colonel, "Did Colonel Tom hire you?"

I wasn't sure how I should answer his question, so I tried to hedge it.

"I'm just here to get a look at Elvis," I said.

I could tell my comment didn't satisfy Red's curiosity, but it would have to do for the time being. I didn't know what the Colonel had told the guys, if anything, and I sure didn't want to be the one to let the cat out of the bag.

Just then the Colonel looked around the room and did a head count. He motioned for Vernon who walked over to him with a clip board. The Colonel checked it and nodded his head in a positive manner.

"You're all wondering why I called you here today, I'm sure; so I'll get right on with it. I called you here because you are the buffer zone between Elvis and anyone outside this circle of friends. Well, you're in for a surprise...a pleasant surprise I hope.

"Before you witness this you will be asked to sign a certificate; actually it is a promissory note for one million dollars to ensure your silence concerning what you are about to learn. If you violate that trust, you will be required, by law to pay the sum I just mentioned. Anyone not willing to sign this agreement and adhere to its conditions...please leave the premises now. If you leave you will not be allowed to be near Elvis again," the Colonel said as he looked sternly around the room.

"I must warn you that this is a very serious matter. If you stay here, you must take this action I've just described," the Colonel reiterated.

The room was as silent as a graveyard for a moment and the faces were as grim as those attending a funeral. Then a slight murmur began to work its way through the crowd.

I knew what was coming, but the promissory note thing had caught me by surprise. Knowing the Colonel though, I should have suspected something like this.

"Vernon please get the signatures of everyone in the room on the documents we had made up before hand," the Colonel said as Vernon Presley began to circulate through the crowd, getting signatures and marking them off on the list he had made of those present. When he got to me, I signed it; after all I was part of the inner circle now.

Once the signatures had been collected and the Colonel was satisfied, he prepared them for what was about to happen next.

"Ladies and Gentlemen...I want you to meet Elvis Presley," the Colonel said and held his hand towards the staircase that led to the bedrooms upstairs.

The looks on the people's faces was one of sheer puzzlement as they peered towards the staircase and waited to see the man they had known for years to make his appearance.

No one said anything as Elvis made his descent down the staircase. A few of the guys looked at one another as if to ask, 'So what's this about...it's Elvis'. Their looks changed when Elvis reached the bottom of the stairs and another Elvis walked up beside him, coming from a room near the bottom of the stairs.

There was stunned silence. I looked at the faces of those present again and saw their eyes snapping from one Elvis to the other. Then the questions started flying.

"What's this all about, Colonel? Elvis...uh, what's going on here; whichever one you are," Red West asked in a stunned voice?

It was amazing. You could not tell one man from the other. As the two of them began taking turns answering questions there was no difference in their voices, either. And, it was obvious the two look-alikes were enjoying every minute of it by their infectious giggles.

After everyone had gotten over the initial shock of seeing two Elvis's, the Colonel took over and began to give them the problem in a nutshell.

"I'd like to introduce you all to the 'new' Elvis Presley; also known as Danny Breedlove; also known as Jesse Garon Presley," the Colonel started and then paused before dropping the bomb on the stunned crowd.

"This is an undertaking we've been forced into because of the injury Elvis received to his voice box during the filming of 'Jailhouse Rock' and aggravated by the blow he received during a karate class while in the Army.

"You can see now why you were required to sign the promissory note for a million dollars ensuring your silence on this. If this ever got out it would be devastating. I think you'll agree that we are well on our way to accomplishing our goal of inserting Jesse, or Danny, into Elvis's shoes," the Colonel stated.

"How do you feel about this Elvis," Scotty Moore, one of Elvis's band members asked?

"Scotty, I couldn't be any happier than I am right now. The brother I thought I'd never see has been, well, sort of resurrected and we're going to be working together. I'll let Jesse," Elvis said, and then looked at his brother, "or Danny as he's been called all these years; let you tell you how he feels about this. Go ahead, Jesse."

Jesse looked at Elvis and flashed that little boy smile the world had come to associate with the King of Rock and Roll. It wasn't a 'put on', however, it was his smile as well as Elvis's.

"I have always felt a kinship to Elvis, but thought it was merely because I was a huge fan of his and we looked alike and I sounded so much like him. People thought I was trying to imitate his voice, but I wasn't.

"I'll tell you something else. The two of us actually felt pain the other might be experiencing over the years. Let me give you a for instance.

"When Elvis got hit in the throat filming 'Jailhouse Rock', I actually lost my voice for a full day and it hurt to swallow. It happened again when he was hit while in the Army," Jesse stated.

Everyone listened intently and then Joe Esposito started laughing. When everyone looked in his direction he shook his head.

"I'm still not sure 'which Elvis' said what," he laughed. "No one is going to know because of the change in voice or looks, that's for sure."

Red West added, "A few of the women might be able to figure something out though, Joe," getting a laugh from everyone.

The questions continued to come hot and heavy, and were answered in turn. Eventually I made my way around to where the Colonel was and pulled him off to one side.

"I'm going to cut out, because I might have a clue as to who is responsible for stealing the dental records of Elvis and the medical records of the other stars. I'll give you a call later and give you an update," I said.

"Go ahead, Sean. This thing may go on for hours. I'm sure these boys will get into a partying sense before long and I've got to make sure no one gets 'loose lips'. Keep me posted on your findings," the Colonel said with a grin.

I left the house with a sense of fulfillment that I'd completed the first part of my investigation. I'd found Jesse Garon and the transformation was now fully underway. I had another thought that brought with it a sense of foreboding danger. It was like juggling three bottles of nitroglycerin; one slip and the whole thing could blow you to smithereens.

What lie ahead of me now was locating dental and medical records that had been stolen and trying to figure out the why. It would take some good detective work on my part, coupled with a lot of luck.

As I made my way back to the city I laid out a schedule of stops that I wanted to make. It was obvious to me that this thing involved much more than merely the stealing of personal records of several movie stars. I had the feeling records were merely the tip of the proverbial 'iceberg'. And the truth was, I didn't know how right I was.

To Be Continued...

Look for 'Counterfeit Elvis': Suspicious Minds.

Made in the USA
Lexington, KY
18 August 2013